Published by WWW.LULU.COM

ISBN: 978-1-4303-2350-1

3

CHAPTER-01.

I never intended to become a Private Investigator. It just sort of happened. Life tends to do as it will regardless of what our dreams are. Me? Well I never really had many dreams. Still, for a tough six foot three inch dyke it is not a bad profession.

My name is Xara (rhymes with Sarah and sounds like it starts with a Z). My mother, God love her, gave me that exotic first name simply because our last name is Smith. I think she expected I would be something special. I guess I am, but it usually doesn't feel like it. Oh I was special growing up. Quite special. In fact so special that I often fell asleep softly crying about it.

Starting very early in life I was a good deal taller than average. My mother dragged me from one Doctor to another always convinced that I had some sort of special condition or disease that caused me to be so tall. The good Doctor would tell her that I was perfectly healthy, just tall for my age. Of course that would be after he would run a dozen tests that all required poking me with needles and me walking around in my underpants in front of him and his nurses.

Dear Mother, of course, would never accept the answer that I was healthy, just tall, so after a few weeks she would find some other doctor we hadn't seen yet and we would repeat the process.

My height caused me a lot of problems when I was young. For instance, I was labeled a problem child. I had no problems at all but the adults around me needed some education. I mean when I was four years old I was as tall as an average six-year-old. Every adult would simply expect me to behave like I was six but I wasn't. I was four, duh!

When I started school, I was not only taller than every girl in class but also taller than every boy in class. You think that made me a target? Sure did.

Of course there were some advantages to being tall. Starting in fourth grade and continuing all the way through high-school I was on the girls volleyball team and the girls basketball team, was the captain of each team, and let's not be humble here – the star of each team. Height wasn't the only advantage I had in sports. God made me tall but I made me strong and fast. I did these with a lot of hard work. I do not know what you spent your allowance and babysitting money on, but I saved up and bought a set of weights with mine. The time other girls spent on the phone or in front of a TV or gossiping with some friends I spent pumping iron or jogging in the hills around our small-town Arkansas neighborhood.

The worst part was that if you could look past my height I was a really pretty and very nice little girl. Like most young ladies I did not consider myself pretty but looking back at the few pictures I can find I have to say that I was a doll. By the time I got to high-school it was pretty clear that I was always going to be taller than most girls, but the boys were starting to catch up. Our high-school had students for four years. As a freshman I was asked out by Junior and Senior boys all the time. Of course I turned down the dates. Surely my parents would not have allowed me to date older boys, but it never really came down to that. I just wasn't interested.

What really pissed me off though was the girls. I mean practically every girl has a best friend growing up. Even those that move into town half way through high-school were able to join some click or something. I lived in the exact same house from the day I was born till after high-school. I always went to the closest public school to my house, so I graduated with several dozen kids that I had done twelve years of school with yet not a single one was ever my best friend. During the sports seasons I got a lot of respect, but never friendship. I do not ever remember spending the night at a friends house. I can remember only three classmates birthday parties that I attended and all three invited everyone in class. I guess with the girls I was just too big and too pretty. At least that is the way I remember it.

About the middle of my junior year I accepted a date from a senior. It was to a school dance. My mother made it a way bigger deal than I did. Yes it was fun to dress up, but I spent all night, I mean every single minute of the date, trying to keep this ass-hole's hands off me. So much for my first date. I quickly followed that date with three or four other first dates and they all were pretty much the same. My senior year went by rather quickly with college scouts graciously watching the girls game at 6:00 P.M. when they were actually in town to scout the senior boys later that night. I did have a date to prom. Lost my virginity that night just because I was tired of guarding against it. The boy was nothing special. I still remember his name but I can't seem to remember much else about him.

How unfair life is finally dawned on me during the last half of my senior year of high-school. I had just spent the last nine years being the most dominant player in two sports. I had more trophies on my mantle than the boy they named "Athlete of the Year" at the awards banquette. Without a doubt I was the best athlete in the school and could whip the ass of any student male or female. All of that and I didn't receive a single scholarship offer. Not one. Several of the boy jocks would escape this dusty little town, but not me because I was dumb enough to be born without dangly parts.

Eighteen, a high-school graduate, no money for college. There were three choices. Choice one, marriage, ha ha ha. Choice two, the wonderful world of community college. I went with choice three, I joined the United States Navy. In our town the recruiting offices are all crammed together on the second floor of a strip mall. Why the Navy? Well, to tell the truth, I had all intentions of joining either the Army or the Marines that day, but when I walked up there the Navy office had a mannequin in the window of a tall blonde woman in a cool blue uniform. Hey, I told you I am a blonde.

So I was actually in the Navy for six years. I won't bore you with the details of how I got there but I ended up working Shore Patrol in San Diego. This was back in what we refer to as the Reagan years. San Diego has always been a big navy town. The 80's were no different. What was different was the military itself. It was changing. It was no longer a male only world. Women could now have real jobs. I had taken a few classes on military science and police science and worked my way through a grueling training regimen to become the closest thing the navy has to cops, shore patrol. I was the only woman of my graduating class but there were other female SPs when I got the assignment.

I had been in the Navy for three years, working shore patrol for two, and had just turned 22 years old when I found out I was a lesbian. It actually came as a big shock to me. I mean here I was this big butch looking military cop surrounded by a million men in uniforms when one of my fellow feminine officers hit on me. Surprise, surprise, surprise. I never fell in love with her but I sure did fall in lust. As far as the military was concerned it was "Don't ask, don't tell", so life as an SP just went on. I didn't stay with the same girl, but from that time forward all of my very few sexual experiences have been with women.

Of course it ended up costing me a career. Some guy found out, and took some pictures and used them as evidence. He didn't have anything against me. He was trying to get back at the other girl in the pictures. Oh well. I resigned the Navy before the Navy resigned me. So I moved to Dallas just to get the hell out of San Diego.

I rented an apartment in the suburb called "Irving" which is right near the airport. I think I chose to live near the airport just in case I had to get out of Dallas as quick as I had left San Diego.

Once in Dallas my first order of business was to find a job. My plan was to find just about any job at all and then start thinking of going back to school. It didn't turn out that way though. I got a job at a legal firm because I had a lot of law and order type training and I could type fast and accurate. If it had been a great big law firm I never would have gotten out of the typing pool but at the small firm I was working at I got a couple of breaks. The first one was that one of the partners had a son my age who was making a living by doing investigations for the clients of the law firm. He mostly trailed around taking pictures of husbands who didn't know it yet but were about to get divorced.

The second break was that this investigator liked me. He kept hitting on me and my big beautiful blondeness and I wasn't quite sure I could tell the son of the boss I wouldn't date him because I was gay. So eventually I agreed to go out with him if it was just to share take-out while he was on a stake-out.

We got along fine and he found out that I knew more about his line of business then he did. I mean the navy had trained me in all the equipment he was using and given me some very extensive self-defense training and weapons work. Plus, I usually helped him figure out what to do next on a case, and I guessed right more often than guessing wrong.

After about half a dozen take-out stake-out dates I was officially assigned to work with him and didn't have to spend the day typing. Of course he still thought he was going to get into my pants. I guess it is a good thing he wasn't too bright.

After a year of playing his assistant I went and got my own PI license. Again my Navy career helped a lot. Because of the Navy I already knew how to fill out tons of paperwork and I knew way more about weapons then the idiot teaching the weapons safety course I was required to take. During that first year with the law firm I stayed in my apartment and had saved up the grand sum of $600.00. Now though, being paid a good deal more because I was licensed, I started really stashing away some cash because I had a plan. I did not want to live the rest of my life in an apartment and I also did not want to live the rest of my life depending on a paycheck from someone else. I wanted a house I could buy and own, but I also wanted to start my own private investigation business.

I knew I would never qualify for a mortgage without a steady pay check though, so I continued to work for the legal firm for three more years and lived like a pauper until my bank account was a healthy 25K+.

At that time I bought a house in Irving and moved in. Three months later, after all the paperwork was filed away and the bank lost interest as long as I made the mortgage payment on time, I quit my job and Dallas County noticed a new business registered at the County Clerks office called "Xara Smith Discrete Investigations."

The house itself was pretty cool. It had originally been built in the 1950s as part of a family oriented block in North Irving. It was originally a three bedroom two bathroom house with a living room, dining room, kitchen, bathroom, and mud room on the first floor, and three bedrooms and a second full bath on the second floor. In addition it had something few north Texas houses had and that was a full basement. I had heard people talk for a couple of years about the land masses that all come together in the area making a very unstable mix for the foundations that almost guaranteed that a basement would leak a lot if you had one there but I had the basement inspected before I bought the place and the inspector told me it hadn't ever had any problems.

Over the years the house had changed but not as much as the neighborhood. In the late 1960s the DFW area built it's shiny new airport half-way between Dallas and Fort Worth, and they certainly needed some new highways to get too and from it. Highway 183, also known as Airport Freeway, plowed it's way through the little neighborhood and the house I would buy had been left facing the highway with a driveway that cut off of the service road running east alongside the highway. The house was approximately halfway between two exits, and it was because of this that I really wanted the house. You see it was zoned for either residential or commercial use so I could legally live in the house and also legally use it as an office for my business, plus it made locating my business easy as long as you could get on a major freeway that connected with 183.

The previous owner had sold golfing equipment for about six years out of the house and I learned it had been a coin shop which also sold comic books before that. To accommodate these businesses, the wall between the living room and dining room had been removed making the first floor dominated by one large room and a decent sized kitchen. The small bathroom was still quite nice and the mud room easily held a washer and drier. But the best thing that had been done was that one of the previous owners had built a back porch and then later enclosed it with an aluminum frame and screens which were eventually replaced with a more solid wooden frame structure filled with Plexiglas. It was a wonderful sun porch that ran the entire length of the back of the house and opened onto the small back yard. There was a small built in pool just off the sun porch and I do admit that this girl had snuck more than once, after dark, buck naked, into the pool. Naughty little me.

Now some four years later I was sitting in the living room, or "office" as I thought of it wondering if a job would come along soon. It had been a struggle at first getting that first client through the door and solving the first mystery and getting the first check. From that time on I had desperately tried to keep a balance of eight grand in my savings account. I figured out my bills and with eight thousand dollars I could make six months of mortgage payments and six months of utility payments plus six months on my health insurance so if I got no business at all for six months I needed to have at least eight grand to fall back on. I looked up my balance on my computer and it was just over six thousand. I needed a case.

I did get a little help from time to time with my bills. I mean right now I had a room mate. I had had a few girlfriends over the years and Laura was the current version. She was a full seven years younger than me. She worked as a stripper using the stage-name "StarLight". Spent her nights on a small stage dancing naked in front of men who would occasionally slip a dollar into the elastic band she kept high on her right thigh. After collecting her dollars from hopeful but unfulfilled men she would crawl into bed next to me and give me more physical pleasure in five minutes than most women get in a month. It is not that I had anything against Laura, but I just did not have time right now for a fulltime relationship, so I am afraid poor little Laura was on her way out, and she didn't even know it yet. On the other hand she was contributing a little cash to the household expenses so I couldn't just toss her to the curb. Vaguely I wondered how many of the cheating husband divorce cases I had worked were fueled by the same motivations. I knew other investigators in town and some of them used girls like Laura in their investigations. When a woman suspected her husband was cheating but the investigator couldn't catch him in the act they would occasionally have someone like Laura lure the unsuspecting man into a compromising but well lighted and therefore easily photographable position. I, myself, had never yet opted for this investigative technique, but to all you married guys out there, be advised that it does happen from time to time. If she is young and cute and has no reason at all to be in bed with you, check for two way mirrors on the wall.

Laura and I had recently celebrated Christmas together and just three weeks ago we had gone to a nice New Years Eve party. I really didn't want to end the relationship but I admitted to myself that not wanting to end a relationship was no reason to extend it if it wasn't going to go anywhere after that. I decided to postpone any decisions on Laura for a few days which made me feel really guilty because I knew I was just using her for ready cash and good sex but what the heck.

Well, that is me, Xara Smith Private Investigator. The introduction is done. Let's get on with the story.

CHAPTER-02.

I looked up from the computer when the door bell rang. I wasn't expecting anyone in particular but it was a Tuesday morning just before eleven so my shop was open for business. The sign on the door clearly told the person standing on the front porch to walk right in but the place still looked more like a house than an office so most people did exactly as she did and rang the bell. As I opened the door I got the usual reaction. She was tall for a woman so she was use to looking down on other females, even many males, but with my full six feet and three inches she had to look up to meet my eyes and this always seemed to surprise tall women. Oh well.

I got her into the chair in front of my desk. She was all business. She got right to the point.

"My husband is going to try to kill me. I want to divorce him, before he gets around to it."

She said this calmly, watching my eyes as she spoke. I am sure she wanted to gauge my reaction. I tried to give her little to judge but the words she spoke had a lot of meaning. So simply had she taken control of the interview. I must do something to get control back.

"Coffee?" I asked.

"Please" she answered, "black, artificial sweetener, no cream."

In less than a minute I had returned with two identical coffee mugs. It was easy though to tell the difference. Hers, black and sweet, mine containing no sweetener but a large spoonful of that white powdery artificial creamer. I put the two mugs on my desk and took out my standard contract. It is basically just a form I fill out with a few pertinent details like her name and contact information. In the body of the contract it goes over my fees and there is, at the bottom, of course, a place for us both to sign.

"Have you spoken to the Police?" I asked her.

Smugly she responded "Yes, and they will be happy to investigate after he actually does something illegal. That won't do me much good though as I won't be alive to help in the investigation. That is why I am looking for someone who can investigate before he actually breaks one of the laws of this state."

I told her that before we could go any further we would have to execute a contract so that I would be bound and unable to divulge things she told me similar to client-attorney privilege.

It wasn't really true. I had no legal reason to keep my mouth shut no matter what the contract said. The grand jury could ask me any question it wanted and I would have to answer. The police too could question me and I would have to answer if I wanted to keep my license. Still, I had found in the past that most clients seemed to be more comfortable about talking with me after we had signed a legal looking document.

There were two other reasons though that I wanted to get her name inked on the contract quickly. The first and most pressing matter was that I needed the work and as soon as her name was on the document I would start getting paid my standard fee whether or not I did a thing for her. Secondly, the sooner we went over the contract the sooner we could get it out of the way. There were some things in it that needed to be there, and it would be a real shame to spend a couple of days working on the case and then not be able to agree on a contract, so it simply must be executed before any real effort is put in. One of the clauses in the contract states that in addition to the regular fee and expenses I was also entitled to eight percent of anything she collects for the first year after my working for her if it is a direct result of my efforts while on the case.

What that means is that if some woman hires me to get evidence against her husband, and then if I spend three days following him around taking pictures of him and his girlfriend, and then if the woman uses the pictures in her divorce of the guy, and then if the judge gives her alimony, I will be entitled to not only my fees for the three days work, and my expenses for gas and film and the like, but that I am also entitled to eight cents out of every dollar she collects in alimony for the first year they are divorced.

I really do not like this clause myself but my lawyer had convinced me originally to include it in my standard contract. Since then though I simply explain it to the client and we see what happens. The very first case I ever did using the contract resulted in the woman getting five hundred dollars a month in alimony. Based on the alimony then I was entitled to forty dollars each month from her if her ex-husband actually paid. She did send me a check every single month but more than half of them bounced so I was spending all my time talking with the bank and running her down for a lousy forty dollars and I ended up doing it month after month for a full year. Generally now when I complete a case I just ignore the clause and never make any attempt to collect my eight percent. Eight percent sounds like such a small amount but the math works out so that if I ever get a case where the judge awards the woman a million dollars as a settlement I will get an $80,000 bonus! Whoopee! Of course, I have not yet had that case.

I started at the top of the contract filling in the date and then asked her what her name was.

Once she told me her name I knew I should have probably recognized her. She was Elizabeth Jenton. For the last ten years she had played second-wife/trophy to Billy Joe Jenton. Billy Joe was the city of Irving's best known divorce attorney. He was sort of in the same business as I was in and, in fact, he had hired me more than once when his case load bulged beyond the abilities of his own private investigators. It was a well worn rumor in town that if a rich woman was getting a divorce, Billy Joe was representing her. The second rumor, supposedly as true as the first, was that about half the wives he represented ended up warming his sheets at night. Proving his infidelity would have been a snap, but she wasn't here for divorce work, she was here for protection. I had to be really careful with this one.

Elizabeth Jenton, or "Betz" as she was better known, had been one of Billy Joe's clients and about a year after her divorce from her first husband which came at the same time as the funeral of the first Mrs. Jenton, the two walked a short aisle in Las Vegas and returned to north Texas as Man & Wife. He had been in his forties then and she had reached the ripe old age of twenty-three. She had inherited Billy Joe's two kids who were a girl, Adrian, seven years old who was already an independent little cuss who claimed she did not want or need a new mother, and a son, Bobby, but called Bubby, who was just four and desperately needed a new mother.

Betz life for the past ten years had been dedicated to three things. The first was getting the kids through school and not in jail without too much publicity. At this time the kids were now a senior and a freshman in high-school with both, of course, still living at home. The second was looking good on Billy Joe's arm when he had to make one of his numerous public appearances. Together they would arrive and then the trophy wives would gather together and chat while the power husbands gathered at some other spot, talked business, and ogled each other's trophies. The third was that she sincerely tried to keep Billy Joe happy with a clean house, good food, and any kind of sex he wanted any time he wanted it. She knew from the start that he was a cheater because that is how they met to begin with, so she had to pretty much ignore his numerous liaisons, but publicly she was a good and loyal wife and privately she made every effort to make the marriage work. Well, at least that is what she was telling me but I knew he would paint a much different picture.

Every investigator in the world knows that nobody tells 100% of the truth. It is not so much that people tend to lie on purpose, but they always present the facts that make them look good and seem to overlook the facts that cast a shadow on their character. A good investigator will interview the wife and then interview the husband and know that the truth lies somewhere in between their two separate versions.

I gathered all the information and went over the terms of the contract. Before signing it she asked what I would do to keep her safe during the course of my investigation. I asked her if she were still living with Billy Joe and what precautions she was taking herself. She told me that she had moved out about a week ago and was living with another woman. She was quick to tell me that there was nothing going on romantically in her life at all. No boyfriends, no dates. The woman she was living with was a person she had met while working on a charity event a year and a half ago and they had been friends and charity workers ever since. I got the address and phone number.

I asked if she had recently, or ever in the past, hired a body guard or guard service. She told me that Billy Joe and the other residents living in the neighborhood where their house was subscribed to a guard service that basically kept a squad car full of armed guards cruising the neighborhood, but other than that she had never been guarded by professionals.

I suggested that she certainly should consider hiring a pro to protect her while my investigation proceeded and offered to make the arrangements. Without asking me the cost of such a service she agreed to have me take care of the details and asked me to set it up as quickly as possible.

I hurried through the paragraph that told her my rates were $400.00 per day plus expenses plus 8% of what she collected. She did not question a thing or even bat that old proverbial eye lash. We both signed and she wrote me out a check for three thousand as a retainer against my first few days working for her and, of course, to pay the guards I hired for her. I also advised her not to contact her husband for any reason at all and that I would personally bring the guard by that I hired for her as soon as I got it set up. I gave her my cell number and watched as she put it in her cell phone. With that done I asked her to tell me why she thought Billy Joe was going to kill her.

Betz told me that she had actually heard Billy Joe talking on the phone and tell someone else that he was going to kill her. I asked for more detail. She lit a second cigarette, took in that first long puff, held it in for a few seconds, then blew out a long stream of second-hand smoke.

"I play tennis every Tuesday at the club" she started. "My partner and I have the indoor court reserved for 10:00 till 11:00 A.M. We usually play for an hour, and then eat lunch at the club and then maybe shopping or a movie so I usually leave the house at nine on Tuesday mornings and don't get back home till two or three. I know the guys that play Tuesdays from 9:00 till 10:00 and they are both a lot better than I am so I like to get there in time to watch most of their match before playing mine, so last Tuesday, which was January 10th, I said good bye to Billy Joe as he headed into the office and then put on my tennis outfit and headed for the club. I got there about 9:15 or so and sat in the bleachers watching the guys play. About 9:45 my partner called my cell and told me she was sick and wouldn't be able to play. I gathered up my stuff and went by the pro shop to cancel our reservation. I drove back home and was surprised to find Billy Joe's car in the driveway. I wasn't trying to be quiet or anything but he apparently did not hear me come in. I had entered the house by the back door that leads into the kitchen and found him sitting there at his desk in the den which he uses as an in-home office. He was facing away from the door and still didn't know I was there. A naughty little idea popped into my head and I backed into the kitchen. I quietly removed my tennis outfit leaving it there on the floor of the kitchen. I got out two glasses, filled them each with wine, and headed quietly back to the den to see if I could, you know, distract Billy Joe from his phone call. As I approached he was still facing away from the door. I snuck a little closer and that is when I heard him clearly say 'With Betz dead I won't have to pay her off or give her any alimony'. Well my heart just froze. I mean there I was naked ready to jump his bones in the middle of the day and he was sitting there talking about killing me. I backed out of the den and put the two wine glasses down on the counter in the kitchen. I grabbed my clothes from the floor and my purse and didn't even get dressed until I was out in the driveway behind our house. I got in the car, got the hell out of there, and just drove around for a while. At three o'clock I drove by the house, saw that Billy Joe's car wasn't there, went inside, packed two suitcases of clothes and jewelry and left. I went directly to the house of my friend where I am staying, then called the police. That was a week ago today, and here I am."

This was going to take a while. I asked Betz if she liked Asian food and then I ordered delivery. While we were waiting for the food I made a call to a friend at one of the guard services and got 24x7 body guards set up. The trouble is that they don't just have a dozen big tough guys sitting bored in a closet waiting for an assignment. The guard service was going to have to arrange some schedules but promised they could have the first shift by my office at 5:00 P.M.

Next I got out a couple of other official looking documents and we filled these in. The way things are today most companies are pretty tight lipped about giving out information but with a waiver signed by Betz I was sure the doctors and hospitals would allow me to copy the Jenton family medical records without a warrant. I might not ever need to see these records, but I had once solved a case and kept my client out of jail by looking at past medical records and proving the victim in that crime could not have sustained the injury he was claiming my client had caused, so I always asked for this medical waiver. There was an additional reason I would need these. I certainly did not wish to alarm Betz, but the medical waiver she had just signed also allowed me to require the state to perform an autopsy on her body should she be found dead even if her husband opposed the autopsy. I found that by asking for a medical waiver for each family member it distracted the client from thinking about what they were signing for themselves. She also signed waivers, at my request, allowing me to look into her credit cards and bank accounts. Hopefully she and Billy Joe would hold joint accounts but knowing Billy Joe there would be several accounts that did not have her name on them.

I asked her about the friend she was staying with. In her opinion Billy Joe would not know this person at all, and would not know how to get in touch with her, Betz, except through her cell phone. She admitted he had called her cell several times but she had not answered any of his calls. He had last tried to contact her that way on Sunday. He had left messages and she played them back for me but they all seemed to be truly just a husband looking for his missing wife.

The Fort Worth/Dallas area is a huge metropolis but the city of Irving, although right in the middle of that metropolis, is still a small town. I felt that it would be a good idea to stash Betz in another suburb. I approached this by suggesting that she was putting her friend in great danger and she did not argue at all. I have some really good friends, Dutch and AJ, who live in a suburb called Arlington which is just south and west of Irving. Laura and I were at their house just the month before exchanging Christmas presents. I had noticed that the house next door to them had a for rent sign out in front. I dialed AJ's phone and she was kind enough to give me the number on the sign. I called the realtor and made an appointment to see it at 2:30. Yes it was available and yes, if I brought my checkbook we could rent it on the spot. The biggest problem was that it was completely unfurnished. The one thing I had wanted though was that it had a garage. I wanted Betz's car stashed. We would rent her a ride if she needed to get around but I put that off because the guard service might be able to provide a car with their guard.

The food arrived and we got to the business of chowing down. We were two tall strong women and there were no men around so we left our manners at the door and attacked the grub.

I gave Betz the address and directions to the rental house in Irving and followed her there in my car without incident. I took her next door and introduced her to AJ and we sat in AJ's living room looking out the window waiting for the realtor who was about ten minutes late. The house was a nice three bedroom three bath room and was way more house than we actually needed but at least it would do for the purposes of stashing Betz and I felt it would be nice to have her close to AJ, someone I knew and trusted. Betz didn't argue when I filled out the lease in my name and she also said nothing when I handed the realtor my corporate platinum to pay the rent. I did make it clear to her after the realtor left that she was paying for the rental but that we did not want to leave a paper trail her husband could follow. I called the guard service and told them the address and told them to have the first guard show up there at 8:00 P.M. and be prepared to stay all night.

With Betz's car stashed safely in the garage and my car parked in AJ's driveway we piled into AJ's car and headed for one of those furniture rental stores. We rented two bedroom sets, a living room set complete with TV and stereo, and a dining room table and chairs. Again my platinum took a big hit and we even paid extra to get it delivered right now. We watched as they loaded up a big truck and followed it back to the rental. It didn't take them long to get everything unloaded and set up. Betz complained that we didn't have cable. Not much I could do about it right then but I did promise to do something about it the next day. With the house basically set up but bare we three women piled into AJ's Amanti and headed for Wal-Mart.

Betz wouldn't admit it but I am sure this was her first ever trip to Wally World. Still we went up and down every single aisle and loaded up on all the things you need in a house. I mean we needed shower curtains and rugs and toilet paper and dishes and pots and pans and shampoo and on and on and on and that didn't even include the food we bought. In addition Betz had basically the clothes she was wearing and the few things she had packed in haste when she had fled Billy Joe. We had to get her a few outfits and new undies. We checked out with three full carts and as spacious as the Amanti's trunk was we still had to ride home with AJ driving, Betz comfortably riding shotgun, and me crammed in the back seat with about a hundred bags.

We pulled into the driveway and immediately there was a problem. I mean I did not want Betz to be seen around the neighborhood so once she was in the house I wanted her to stay there, and AJ, God love her, has a little problem walking too much and I had already sent her all the way through Wal-Mart, so that meant that yours truly had to unload the whole car and carry all the stuff inside the house. We had only unloaded about seven or eight bags of stuff when we spotted a big problem. The house had no refrigerator. I hadn't noticed before. There was a really nice stove, and a built-in microwave, but no fridge. Once again though it was AJ to the rescue. About a year ago AJ had bought a new fridge herself and had put her old one in her garage because I told her I wanted it and here a year later I still had not picked it up. Well thankfully her husband, Dutch, was just pulling into the driveway so he helped me wrestle the box across the driveway and into the new kitchen.

I have to admit once I got the bags inside the door Betz really took over putting the stuff away. I mean if I were in her place I would be all worried and scared and thinking my life was over and wallowing in self pity but she was spritzing around like a teen-ager who was setting up for her first slumber party. She actually seemed happy in the manual labor of setting up a new household.

Exhausted, I sat my ass down at the dining room table and pulled out a steno pad and a pen. I started making notes including the massive expenses I had already gone through. My notes were pretty copious. I have always found that if I wrote everything down I could always trim it down later, but if I did not write it down when it was fresh then I would loose it for ever.

The guard arrived and I introduced him to myself, Betz, AJ, and Dutch. He went by the name Bear, and that is what was on his company ID card. I had expected as much because I had worked with his agency before. Their guards were all given false names and it was the only name the actual client ever got. It was their attempt to keep the guard separate from the people he was guarding, keep him as a guard and keep him from becoming a friend. It was important that he be allowed to do his job and not be encumbered with emotions like friendship. Bear was my height and about 290 pounds of solid muscle. His skin was darker than any flesh I had ever seen. His head was shaved. His smile was savvy and his pearly whites glowed like a million stars. He was polite but also very self confident. He looked fabulous in his uniform which was tailored to fit like a glove, and he had a large silver 44 strapped to his waist. I took two quick short breaths and immediately started reconsidering my commitment to lesbianism.

Together Bear and I made a circuit around the house from the outside and then we checked every window and door making sure all were locked. I shooed Dutch and AJ home thanking them copiously for their help. I made sure Betz put Bear's phone as well as Dutch and AJ's in her cell phone, but warned her not to call unless there was a serious problem. I told her not to answer her phone unless it was one of us but told her to leave it on so she could get messages. I would be curious to see what her hubby would say if he called. At her insistence I allowed Betz to call the woman she had bunked with for the past week and let her know that Betz was safe but not coming back. I promised to meet them there at the house the next day in the morning, and left them to play house.

When I got to my own humble abode Laura was there and we sat down and had a nice conversation. I let her know what my newest case was all about but was very careful to not tell her who was involved. I worked about an hour putting my notes in order and filing away my receipts then sat in a bubble bath for thirty minutes. It didn't take me long to fall asleep that night.

CHAPTER-03.

Early Wednesday morning I made a list of the people I wanted to talk to. The first step would be to gather some background information but my primary clue at this point was the phone call Betz had overheard. I certainly wanted to find out who Billy Joe had been speaking to so that became the first action item. There was a lot more though that I wanted to find out. For instance, why was Billy Joe at their home at all? According to Betz's story Billy Joe had left the house at his usual time dressed for the office where she assumed he was going. He knew she had the Tuesday tennis date. I was curious if he ever got to the office that day or had he left the house and simply awaited for her to vacate the house and then returned. If so, why? Was this the first time he had been at the house in the middle of the day when he was supposed to be at the office, or was it a habit? To answer these questions I could simply interview his neighbors and co-workers, but I couldn't very well do that without letting him know I was investigating him.

I knew a girl named Mandy that I really did not like very much but I had to put up a good front for fairly often. She was valuable for two reasons: First she worked for the local telephone exchange and second she was very bribable. She was one of those women who just grate on your nerves but doesn't realize it, and therefore she has no friends at all. I have found that if I offered her a little friendship once in a while she would pull luds on just about anything I asked her. Sure I had a signed authorization for Betz, but Billy Joe hadn't signed a thing, and the phones were probably in his name. I spun my rolodex to her number and gave her a call. I caught Mandy at her desk and told her what I was after. She promised she could have the info ready by the end of the day so I had to invite her to dinner at my house followed by her passion which was a couple of rounds of scrabble. In the past couple of years I had cheated to loose several times trying to keep her in the game, but she thought she was good at it. Oh well. Since it was getting so close to the end of the day, and I had a few other things to get to I put Mandy off till the next evening and set up a Wednesday night date for lasagna and scrabble at my house.

That piece of business done I called the local cable company and found that they wouldn't even have to visit the house unless I needed new wiring. I paid the deposit over the phone and they threw a couple of switches or whatever they do and I told them I would call back if I needed any wires run through the house.

It was raining when I locked the house/office and ran to my six year old Taurus. It fired right up and I put some old Lynard Skynard on the CD player. I headed west on 183 till it hooked up with 360 and headed south into Arlington. I got off one exit early and dashed into my favorite bakery where I picked up a dozen of the best bagels in the world thinking it would make a nice breakfast for everyone. Fat chance.

I pulled into the rental where I had stashed Betz. When I walked in the door Betz was sitting at the dining room table with Bear's replacement, Tiger, who could have been Bear's clone and the first thing that popped into my mind was "I wonder how much it would cost to collect the entire set". AJ was there and she was at the stove. I walked in just as she was loading up plates for Betz and Tiger who were comfortably seated at the table. I poured myself a cup of coffee and before I got to the table AJ put a plate down for me. The sausage and eggs were delicious. I do not remember buying any hash browns at Wal-Mart but there they were on my plate. Yum.

I tried to conduct a little business while we ate the feast but nobody wanted to stop chewing long enough to talk. Finally, over a second round of coffees I went over the schedule with Tiger and set some ground rules for him and Betz. I wanted Betz protected but I wanted it to be as little like living in prison as I could make it. Therefore I did not forbid them from leaving the house but insisted that they not go to Irving, not go anywhere where they were likely to run into anyone Betz usually hung out with, and always traveled in disguise. This did not mean radically changing Betz physically, it simply meant she would wear a scarf and sun glasses when not in the house. Reluctantly I handed Tiger a copy of my credit card. I did not want Betz to leave any paper trail at all, but I made it clear to her that my credit limit was nothing like what she was used to.

I shooed AJ home and then tested my technological skills by hooking up the cable to the TV we had rented. Fortunately it worked on my first try because one try was all my skills would have permitted.

Betz and I then sat down and had a long conversation. I wanted to get a good idea of the daily life and schedule followed by Betz and Billy Joe. One thing particularly bothered me. According to Betz she had left home a week ago, and I had heard nothing of it at all. I mean Billy Joe and Betz were the media darlings of Irving Texas. Why had I not read any news stories of a missing socialite? Why had the police not broadcast an adult version of the Amber alert? Other than calling Betz cell phone what had Billy Joe done to try to find her?

I questioned Betz about her disappearance and if it had happened before. She actually started crying during this conversation. The previous day when she had walked into my office she appeared strong and tough and aloof. Now she appeared more like a scared little girl. Apparently she no longer felt the need to put on a front for me and she felt free to let her emotions out. Her answers assured me that this was the first time she had ever been away from Billy Joe since their marriage. There had been a couple of times over the past years when Billy Joe had been away for a week-end hunt or fishing trip with some good old boys, but in those cases she had been at home with the kids and he had called her each night and he had been where he had said he would be and he had come home when he was supposed to come home. He had stayed late at the office way more times then he needed to and she recognized that these late nights often occurred at the apartment of some other woman rather than the office, but he always came home even if it was late. She had no idea why he would want her dead, she had simply heard him talking about it and had fled. I am sure there was more to the story she was telling me but she gave me what she was comfortable with and I didn't press to hard.

I ended up with very little of what I really wanted which was Billy Joe's schedule. His job simply was not a nine to five gig. He did leave the house Monday through Friday in the morning, but a good deal of his legitimate business would be conducted in places other than his office. She could never count on him being home at dinner time, but she didn't exactly spend a lot of time cooking dinners for him either. No matter how I worded the question she kept weaving the answer so that it ended with her trying to be a good little wife who was very forgiving and constantly ready to keep him satisfied. I finally realized that she knew a lot about how she and Billy Joe got along when they were together but she really knew very little about what he did when he was not at home with her. Even when I asked about some of the appearances they made together she gave the impression that she was playing the part of the bauble on Billy Joe's arm rather than playing the part of Betz Jenton. She would focus on looking good and behaving like a socialite in front of the cameras and it didn't matter to her whether it was a political rally or an opera. Her job was to look good for her man and show the world they were a happily married couple who loved each other and took their job as parents seriously. I tried to press her about Billy Joe's recent clients. It would be a matter of public record to look up the trials he had been a part of but I also knew that a lot of his clients ended up settling things before they actually got to trial so there might not be any official record of these clients. Betz could give me very little about who the recent clients were but she did let slip that lately they were not all divorce cases. According to Betz, Billy Joe had done a lot of work recently for a couple of big real estate people.

It was time for me to go to work. I could have justified staying with Betz all day and protecting her from harm for another twenty-four hours, but that is why I had hired her the guard service. My job was to find out if there was any real danger to the woman and if so figure out a way to make that danger go away.

I said good-bye and hopped in my car. As I pulled out of the driveway I noticed AJ peeking out her front window. She would probably be back with Betz before I got to the end of the block. I said a silent prayer that I hadn't placed my good friend in danger.

It was almost noon on Wednesday so I stopped at Joe's Coffee Shop. In Irving this is the place that the old timers gather and many of them fondly remember being there with their parents years before. More deals were consummated here at Joe's than any office in Irving. The coffee was delicious, the waitresses flirted, and the gossip was spoken not whispered. There is always a bunch of business men there and the back of the restaurant was usually filled with real-estate folks talking about the market being about to turn in their favor. I was sort of hoping that Billy Joe would be there but he was not.

The talk at Joe's revolved around two things this day. Both had to do with the Dallas Cowboys. I had picked out a table in the middle of the long dining room. To my north, where all the commoners were sitting, the talk was centered around the upcoming playoff game. Dallas had not actually won a playoff game in nine years but with a record of 9 and 7 they would host the Philadelphia Eagles this Sunday at Texas Stadium, which is actually in Irving. Most of the talk was about how they would forcefully march through the playoffs one game at a time and then play in the Super Bowl. I was tempted to get on this bandwagon and really pull for the Cowboys, but if I were a betting woman I would have placed a yard on the Eagles. There were two different men sitting in that end of the restaurant that I recognized as attorneys. As far as I could remember neither of them were exactly friendly with Billy Joe, and both of these men were sitting at full tables so it would be hard to just barge in on them. I decided to leave them alone for now.

To my south, at the back of the restaurant, where the real estate people had gathered, they were talking about the new stadium. The Cowboy's were building a new stadium in Arlington and it was at the stage of the project where they were buying up the land and scheduling the first game there for three years in the future. It was a very important topic to the real estate folk, every one of which had figured out a way to make him or her self rich on the deal and very willing to tell everyone else their idea. There was a guy there who I knew only as Clive. I do not think I had ever met him in person but his face was on billboards all over town advertising the real estate agency he owned. They had some maps out on the table and somebody was pointing to a track of land facing the proposed sight of the new stadium but not an actual part of the stadium sight. In other words this would be the land across the street from the new stadium once it was built. Some guy was saying that buying up some of that land would be a good investment because there would have to be a lot of development in that area for sports bars and night clubs and probably even pro shops selling Cowboy jerseys at four times the going rate on game days. It was Clive who said "That would be an excellent suggestion but Billy Joe already has an option sewed up on those tracks."

I didn't learn anything else at Joe's but I would include Billy Joe's interests in Arlington to my notes. I had just moved Betz to Arlington to get her out of his domain and already I had found that his business tentacles reached that town as well. I probably should have expected as much.

I stopped at a grocery on the way home. I had to prepare for my scrabble date with Mandy tonight. I wasn't much looking forward to it but the luds from Billy Joe's phones would provide a lot of information and save me a lot of leg work. There were no guarantees, but I felt the risk well worth the potential reward. My girlfriend Laura worked every Friday night and every Saturday night and then one or two nights during the week. She never made much money on the week nights, but if she wasn't willing to put in some time during the week they wouldn't let her on the schedule for the week-ends. I hated waking her but needed to know if she were going to be home that night so I buzzed her on my cell from the grocery parking lot. She giggled a lot at my needing to perform the humiliating task of pretend friendship to Mandy, so she promised to be there. "Wouldn't miss it for the world" were her exact words.

I picked up a frozen lasagna that could feed a football team, and a couple of loafs of French bread. One thing I hate about Irving is that it is dry. I mean bone dry. You can't even buy beer or wine at the grocery stores here, and there is not a single liquor store in the town. I nudged the Taurus across the border into Dallas and stopped at the first liquor store. I grabbed three bottles of cheap white wine and headed back to my office/house.

Laura was up and moving around when I got there. She was sitting at the kitchen table drinking coffee in her maids outfit. Her maids outfit is a skimpy little apron worn over her birthday suit. She wears it to tempt me but actually does most of the house cleaning in it as well. It is kind of fun to watch her vacuum. I guess my life doesn't totally suck.

"Planning a little domestic engineering, my dear?" I asked.

"Just trying to lure you into the shower, Ma'am" she responded.

What the hell, I felt a little grimy.

A couple of hours later we popped the lasagna in the oven and went about actually cleaning the house. It didn't take us long. I forced Laura to put clothes on and she promised to be on her best behavior, but she winked as she was crossing her heart. It was not going to be pretty.

Mandy arrived at 6:30 on the dot. Punctuality was one of her good points. The first thing she did was hand me a big thick envelope crammed with paper which I knew would be Billy Joe's phone records for the last three months. I was so tempted to set the kitchen on fire so we would have an excuse to send Mandy home early, but like a good little friend I welcomed her into my home and we settled down to a nice evening of friendship, even though it was forced.

Mandy knew Laura from a couple of previous scrabble parties. We wrestled the lasagna onto the table and unscrewed the first wine bottle. Dinner was fabulous. Quickly we cleared the table and got the scrabble board set up. Of course we kept pouring the wine while we played. Mandy started things off with the word "border". I played second and used her "B" to spell the word "bring". Laura giggled and used my "I" to spell the word "lick". I could tell how this game was going to go.

We ended up playing four separate games and I won't bore you with a play-by-play with every word we used but I will recap a few things for you. Keep in mind we were guzzling wine the entire time. Laura did surprisingly well and actually won the first two games while constantly finding ways to spell naughty sounding words. A sample is "wiggle, nude, oral, spank, leather, shaved, boobs," and three different words that end in "uck". Yes I know you immediately thought of two of the words and you are correct. The third was "buck". Buck, in itself, is not a dirty word, but she had previously placed the word "naked" on the board, and she added the new letters to spell "bucknaked". Of course we argued that buck naked was two separate words but by then we were all a little tipsy so we allowed it.

As hard as I tried to let Mandy win, I accidentally won the third game, so it looked like Mandy might go home disappointed. That all ended at the end of the fourth game. Apparently Mandy had drawn the blank tile early in the game and had saved it throughout, then on her very last play of the game she used the blank as the letter "Z" so she could spell "lezzie", and it landed on a double-word score so she kicked our asses that game. We all laughed at that one and it just naturally ended scrabble for the evening.

We did the responsible thing and took Mandy's car keys from her. Quickly Laura checked the guest bedroom and we picked something to watch on the television. Laura and Mandy settled on the sofa so I took the big barko-lounger. Laura drizzled the last of the three bottles of wine into our glasses. I reclined the chair to get comfortable. I have no recollection of what we were watching on TV.

CHAPTER-04.

When I woke up it was light outside. Someone had tossed a blanket over me. My back was stiff and sore from sleeping in the recliner. I started the coffee pot and got out the envelope Mandy had brought me. I decided to take a quick shower while the coffee was brewing and then settled down to my desk in my big fluffy robe with Billy Joe's phone records.

I worked diligently for three hours pouring over the phone details. I made a lot of notes, pages of them. I was hard at work when I heard someone else hop into the shower. Several minutes later Mandy, fully dressed but with wet hair, blew through the room. She quickly thanked me for the fun evening, blew me a kiss, told me to call if I needed anything else, and headed out the door.

Billy Joe and Betz had a total of five voice phones and two dedicated fax lines. They had a fax at both Billy Joe's office and one at the house. They had two separate voice lines from his office, one line at home, and they each had a cell phone. I had gotten really lucky there because they billed their cell phones with the same company that provided their land lines and it was the company that Mandy worked for. Lately in my business I had often had to chase down luds from several companies to get all the phone records, but who knows, even with what I had Billy Joe could easily have an additional cell phone billed through another company that even Betz might not know about. At any rate, I had a lot of data and a lot to go over. I continued on.

The first thing I wanted to establish was the question about why Billy Joe was at home on that Tuesday when Betz had heard him on the phone in his office. He had left for the office less than two hours earlier, but he knew Betz would be out of the house from about nine till nearly one. Was this the first time he had come home unexpectedly on Tuesdays, or was it a habit?

I separated out the phone details from his home phone line. They had only one home voice land line, but they probably had at least three extensions on that line. I would have no way of knowing which actual phone Billy Joe had used, and, at this point of my investigation it didn't really matter whether he was calling someone from his office or the extension in the kitchen. The point was that he would be making calls from home when he should have been at the office, or at least out of the house. I had call records that went back twelve Tuesdays starting in November and ending the week that Betz overheard her death threat. I did have to ignore two of those Tuesdays because over the Christmas and New Year week everybody's schedule is messed up. So that left ten regular Tuesdays and I found the phone records that proved that there were outbound calls from the home phone on eight of those Tuesdays during the hours that Betz was out of the house. I did have to remember that there were two teen-agers living in the house as well. Either of them could have been using the phone if they were home. I made myself a note to check with their schools and check their attendance on the recent Tuesdays.

On the particular Tuesday in question Billy Joe had dialed four different numbers and, unfortunately, they were all in a time frame compressed enough that I could not be sure who he was talking with when Betz had eavesdropped. So there I had it. I had four numbers that Billy Joe COULD have been talking to when he had mentioned Betz's death. I looked back through the numbers dialed on those previous Tuesdays, and then expanded it to all of the other days and all of the other phones as well. All four numbers were for phones that Billy Joe dialed often and regularly.

Just to be sure I checked Billy Joe's cell phone luds for the Tuesday in question. He had several calls registered that day but none during the time frame I was currently interested in. I started wondering why someone would go through the hassle of making sure they had complete privacy by arranging through subterfuge to be the only person in the house, and then use the land line rather than the cell phone. The truth of the matter is that there are several devices available that are relatively inexpensive, work on radio waves, and are capable of intercepting cell phone transmissions. These devices are still new enough that the courts have not yet had the opportunity to rule on their legality, meaning that they are not yet exactly illegal. On the other hand it takes a court order to tap a land line. Therefore, believe it or not, a land line is safer for the purposes of privacy then cell phones are. Of course, if you do not care who hears it as long as they can't prove it was you who said it then get a pre-paid cell phone. They don't record the luds on those things.

Five years ago I would have needed Mandy for the next step, but this is the age of the internet. I pay eighteen dollars per year to subscribe to a specific service that I use all the time. That comes to about three cents each day. I got on the reverse Cole's directory and poked in the four phone numbers and was rewarded with the name and address of each registered phone number. At that point I had a list of four people, one of which was involved, and the other three who were, for all likelihood, completely innocent of the death threat to Betz. I did not recognize any of the names on my short list.

Time to get up and stretch a little. I poked my head into my bedroom and found Laura there looking like an angel. Sound asleep, naked, on top of the blankets, fetal position, sucking her thumb. It was nearly noon but for a girl that works nights this was her prime sleep time so I left her alone. I poked my head into the guest room expecting to have to clean it up a little and at least make the bed. Apparently Mandy is a good house guest because the bed and room were just as tidy as when we had offered it to her the night before.

I got dressed quietly so as not to disturb Laura. Back at my desk I gave Betz a call. Everything was fine. I asked her if she had skipped any tennis games in the last three months and other than the one where she snuck home to find Billy Joe there, and also other than the ones over the holidays, she had not missed any matches. She also, without my asking, offered up contact information on her tennis partner so that I could verify the info. She thanked me for all the work I had already done securing her safety and told me the rental house was quite comfortable. She also appeared to be enjoying the friendship her new neighbor AJ was providing.

I fired up the Taurus having no real plan other than getting some mileage I could put on my billing statement for Betz. I mean I had already spent three serious hours working on her case this day but most clients can't see sitting at your desk as a billable item but easily equate the mileage receipts into action by the sleuth they have hired. I drove over to a building called "The Appraisal District". It is the government building where the Dallas County real property tax records are kept. I do not know why it is called the appraisal district. At any rate I was immediately shut down on my plan. I had expected to get the current plan for the new stadium so that I could get some idea of which land tracks Billy Joe was buying. It was a good plan except for one thing. Arlington, and therefore the new stadium, is not in Dallas County, it is in Tarrant County. Oh well. Some times I still feel like I am new to the area and once again I better remind you that I am very capable of having a blonde moment or two occasionally. At least I was able to get the location of the building in Tarrant county I would need to visit. I put twenty-four miles on the Taurus getting to down town Fort Worth and finally got a survey map of the new stadium sight.

Keep in mind that I had no idea if the new stadium works had anything to do with my current case but I had to start somewhere. In fact, when I had been in the restaurant and overheard Clive say that Billy Joe had the options on those properties I really had no proof at all that he was talking about Billy Joe Jenton. This is Texas and you can find a Billy Joe under just about every bush. Somehow though I simply felt in my gut that it was my Billy Joe that Clive had been talking about. Why Billy Joe would be getting into real estate near a proposed new stadium was part of the mystery but it was one of the very few possible clues I had to pursue at the time.

Back at the office I tacked the map up on one wall and immediately thought better of it. What if someone walked into my office and saw it there? Wouldn't that tell them exactly what I was working on? I spread the map out on my desk and looked it over. The new stadium sight was clearly noted and at this time all the property had not yet been acquired so none of the construction had begun and it was all still neighborhoods. It was quite impressive how big the area they were marking off was. I had no idea it would take that much space. Of course it was not all for the stadium itself, but also planned was a huge hotel, several other buildings having to do with concession and servicing, it's own electrical power station, a police sub-station including holding cells, and of course, plenty of parking. Add to that roads in and out that would have to be built and I guess it was a massive project meaning there would be a lot of money to be made. I pulled up a map of the current Texas Stadium on my computer for comparison and found that the new one actually wouldn't take up any more space than the old one now occupied. I also started wondering what the old one would be used for after the Cowboys moved and wondered if there was any money to be made on those deals. I expected there was.

I thought I remembered which tracks of land the guy in the restaurant was pointing at that Clive had said Billy Joe had the option for. I really couldn't get it clear in my mind where they were on my new map. I started wondering how I would be able to find out what Billy Joe held options on and then realized that I wasn't even sure what "options" meant in real estate terms.

I put the map away and headed over to the proposed stadium sight to get a close up look. To me it all just looked like neighborhood. Since I was in Arlington anyway I figured I would head over to the rental and see how Betz was doing.

Betz and AJ were watching a movie on cable and Bear had just come on to relieve Tiger. I had no idea how their schedule worked other than one of them would always be present and on duty. Something smelled good and I found out AJ had a pie in the oven. She claimed to be just testing out the oven because she wanted to make sure Betz would be able to use it but I really didn't think Betz would be spending her time improving her baking skills. Bear took me around the perimeter of the house and showed me three windows that needed better locks. He told me what to buy and where to buy them and promised he could install them.

I headed back towards my house in Irving. It was really a beautiful day. This part of north Texas has about four or five days of winter each year and this day wasn't one of them. The sky was clear and the temperature was in the upper sixties. It would plunge all the way down to the forties at night so the heat would definitely be on, but the late afternoon was just plain gorgeous. I was wondering why anyone would want to live anywhere else. I needed some of what I call "fresh air therapy."

I did not take my exit off of 183 but rather headed over to Irving Boulevard and pulled into the lot of the SPCA. I do a lot of volunteer work for the SPCA. They have twenty cages for adult dogs and as sad as it is most of these mutts won't be adopted before their time allotment is up. The SPCA does not put the dogs down when they fail to get adopted, but they do send them to the county pound where their time is then short and fatal. The dogs spend all of their time at the SPCA in their small concrete cages except for when a volunteer comes in and walks the poor animals. The building is small and cramped and even though they keep it as clean as they possibly can, it smells just like you would expect it to. It takes about three minutes the first time you visit to fill out the small amount of paper work which I had done a couple of years ago. From then on all you do is walk in, sign the list, and head into the kennels. Once there you simply pick out a leash, pick out a dog, and head to the big field next door.

I said my hello to Julie who works behind the desk, signed my name to the list of that days volunteers, dropped a fiver into the donation jar, and stepped through the door into the noisy kennel. I picked out an old gal who was a mixture between Dalmatian and something else, probably Black Lab. My new best friend and I went to the empty field with her pulling hard on the leash and me being dragged behind. Once we were clearly in the field and away from the noisy building she stopped pulling so hard on the leash and led the way in a less strenuous manner. In a few moments her bladder had been emptied and I started actually getting a little jealous. I didn't exactly have to pee, but I wondered why every animal on the planet except for humans were permitted to walk around naked all the time and pee when and where they wished without any guilt. We humans, the dominant species on the planet, restrict ourselves to wearing uncomfortable clothing at all times and sneaking into a tiny porcelain closet to relieve ourselves privately. Do these thoughts make me kinky, silly, romantic, sympathetic, weird, or just plain pathetic?

My mutt led me to a beautiful little spot in the field and she sat down. I checked for other doggies droppings and seeing none I sat down next to the regal girl. She waited for me to get comfortable and then she just sort of crawled over and laid across my lap. I stroked her soft silky fur and listened to her loving gurgling. I do some of my best thinking in situations like these.

Statistically the number one reason why a husband kills a wife or a wife kills a husband is money. According to what I knew, or thought I knew, Billy Joe was already quite wealthy and with the real estate he was supposedly buying up near the new stadium, he was set to make a lot of money in the very near future. When men get rich they all seem to want a trophy wife who will look good on their arm in public, take care of their first wife's kids, quietly look the other way when he beds some other woman, and act like a thousand dollar hooker in the bed room. According to the story Betz was telling it would be hard to find a better match for Billy Joe than what he already had in her.

The second most popular reason for spousal homicide is infidelity. If you check out money and sex you clear somewhere near 85 percent of the domestic murders. Betz had admitted she knew Billy Joe was fooling around, and she didn't really like it but appeared to deal with it. She, however, might just not be telling me the whole truth. If she were fooling around on the side, and Billy Joe had found out about it, it could possibly set off the conversation Betz had reportedly overheard. I needed to have a conversation with Betz's tennis partner. With her I could tell her that Betz was missing and I was trying to find her and that would probably motivate the friend into revealing little confidences she might otherwise hide. The other person I needed to have a conversation with was the woman Betz had hidden out with the previous week. She, I would have to handle a little differently. She already knew the truth about where Betz was and why she was there so she would not be convinced by one of my little white lies.

Another thing to consider is that infidelity did not necessarily have to mean that the wife was actually doing anything at all. More than one wife had been murdered when her husband had heard that she was screwing some other guy and then after the murder it was proven that what the husband had heard was simply not true.

I also needed to find a way to get closer to Billy Joe and the business deals he was currently working on. That one would be a bit tricky. It was time to get moving again. When I tried to get up the spotted lady in my lap politely asked for ten more minutes of peace and quiet outside her cage. I had to allow it. Reluctantly though, after that ten minutes had passed, she allowed me to lead her back to doggie prison.

The fresh-air therapy had done wonders for my head. Summing things up I had only been on the case 48 hours and I had Betz stashed away in a place that I felt was probably as safe as I could hope for without getting her all the way out of the state. I had collected evidence that Billy Joe was, for reasons unknown, sneaking back into his own house to use the phone and home office while his wife was out of the house. I had a list of just four people to check out who were the possible people Billy Joe had been speaking to when Betz heard the threat. I had two women to speak with to try to begin my investigation into Betz herself. Also, I had picked up a lead into just what sort of business interests might be currently taking up Billy Joe's time and interest. Not much I admit, but pretty good for just two days work.

On almost every detective movie or TV show I had ever seen the P.I. has a trusted friend on the police force that can get inside info at a crucial time. Not so for this gal. Sure I had met a few cops during my previous investigations but not a single badge owed me a favor. What I needed at the time was to take the list of the four men I had that Billy Joe had talked to that Tuesday morning and get a thorough background on each of these men. If I could figure out which one Billy Joe actually had on the phone at the crucial moment I could eliminate the other three and therefore make my efforts much more likely to pay off. Right now though all I had was their names, phone numbers, and addresses.

At my home I fired up the computer and clicked on that little blue "e" that magically connected me to the internet. I had to get out my secret code book to look up my password to a web site I have a membership on but rarely use. I typed in the four names and also typed in my credit card number. The complete background checks this site provided did not cost three cents a day, they cost seventy-five bucks each. In the past though the data had proved well worth the money. If I had been spending my own money I would have tried a little harder and ranked the four characters using mostly intuition and then paid for their dossiers one at a time, because I knew that three of the four would be, to me, useless, but I wasn't spending my own money and also felt that the expense that Betz was paying for would be easily justified if it helped save her life. The trouble is that even though it is internet based these reports would not be instantaneous. I would give up the four contacts and wait probably three or four hours for my results.

I also took the time to pull out the notes I had made about the Jenton children. One thing I wanted to establish was if either of the children had been missing from school on the Tuesdays that Billy Joe was at home using the phone while Betz was at her tennis match. It might be important and it also might not. It's worth though would never be found if I could not confirm whether they were at school or at the house. I called the principal of the local high-school and was met at first with a brick wall. When I told her I had releases signed by Betz and also releases signed by Billy Joe she softened her stand and eventually an assistant was found who would go over the attendance records for me. I did all this over the phone. I wondered just a little what might have happened if I did not truly have the signed releases. Would I still have been able to talk her into releasing the data? At any rate the assistant assured me that each Jenton child had been present and accounted for on the dates I had asked about. Oh well.

Thursday afternoon was slipping away. Laura was up and moving around somewhere in the back of the house. She would be off to work soon. Shaking her bare bottom and collecting pictures of presidents, mostly Georges. I got the map out again and was pouring over it very studiously when Laura strutted through the office and out the front door with a slight kiss to my cheek. I listened as her car fired up and said a silent prayer that she be safe that night.

Looking back at the map and knowing I was looking at something important but not knowing what it was that I was seeing. Little colored lines representing a great project. One inch equals half a mile. The shrill ring of the phone startled me and I unprofessionally picked it up on the first ring.

"Xara   Smith   discrete   investigations"   I mumbled.
"Hi Xara, this is Billy Joe Jenton."

CHAPTER-05.

WTF?

Stammering, I said "Mr. Jenton? What can I do for you?"

"Oh please" he drawled in his best Texan, "Everybody just calls me Billy Joe."

"Right, er, I mean, yes, Billy Joe, What can I do for you?"

"Well" he said "I've got myself a bit of a mystery that I might just need your help on. Can you come by this evening so we can talk?"

Alarm bells were going off all over the place and I saw a big sign that was flashing the word danger over and over. I opened my eyes and shook my head. I took a short breath willing my voice to not give me away.

"Let me look at my schedule and see when I can make myself free" I said a little less than convincingly.

"Great" he responded completely uninterested in what conflicts my schedule might conveniently provide. "Can you come by my house at seven?"

"Sure, Billy Joe. What is your address?" I countered.

He gave me the address and wrestled away all of my probing questions while artfully getting off the phone.

Now what? I looked at the clock and it was a little after five. I had less than two hours to present myself to the prime suspect in the mystery I was currently working on. What all did he know? Remember, I had worked for Billy Joe a couple of times in the past. Could it be that he already knew that I was working for Betz?

I put on jeans and a t-shirt and laced up my running shoes. I layered a tough looking leather jacket over the shirt. Then I added the armaments. I started by duct-taping a switch-blade inside my left pant leg down by my ankle. I slipped an old but trusted small one-shot derringer in the right pocket of the jacket. I opened my business looking briefcase and took out the false bottom and checked to make sure the colt was there locked and loaded. I slipped a small fresh tube of pepper spray into the tight right back pocket of my jeans. I walked across the room to see if I clanked.

What I needed was a safe call. I wanted to tell someone exactly where I was going and also tell them that if I didn't call them at a certain time saying that I was safe they should call the police and send in the cavalry. I was not about to call Laura. I didn't want her worrying and she would certainly worry if I entrusted her to such a duty. My next thought was to give the rental a call and leave the instructions with either Betz or the guard but there were two problems with that. The first was that I was actually investigating Betz just as much as I was investigating Billy Joe so I didn't want to tip my hand, and the second was that if Betz were totally innocent and truly in danger then I did not wish to appear incompetent to her. I dialed Mandy's number wondering exactly what to tell her but she didn't answer and I certainly wasn't going to leave a message on her answering machine.

Dressed in my tough-girl outfit and loaded down with military hardware I still felt like a naked Christian who was about to be tossed to the lions as I fired up the Taurus and headed over to Billy Joe's house. Not my best professional moment.

The sun had set between Billy Joe's call and my arrival at his den. I was surprised at how dark it seemed and wondered if this girl would see the sun rise once more. I took the time to back the Taurus into a parking space near the front door so that it was poised and pointed if I needed a quick get-away. I rung the bell and heard it toll. I forced panic down waiting for him to answer the door. Soon though he did with a big professional smile hung over a thousand dollar Italian suit.

It was the nicest house on the block. Hell, it was the nicest house I had been in, in two years. The entry hall was large and marbled. A grand staircase led to the second floor and half way up was a landing that my house would have fit on. Off to the left was a very well appointed living room. To the right was a spacious hall that led past his office and into the kitchen. Billy Joe led me into his office and put a drink in my hand without even asking if I wanted one. I took a big sip not realizing how parched I was. He sat at the chair behind his desk and motioned for me to take one of the chairs across the desk from him. Trying to appear calm, and willing my heart to beat less loudly, I lowered my terrified ass into a leather clad club chair. It was probably a very comfortable chair but I really have no recollection of comfort at the awkward moment.

I noticed that I had placed my briefcase on my lap. I slowly took another sip of my drink, bourbon and water I think, and placed the glass on the edge of his desk right in front of me. Slowly I slid my right hand into the pocket of my jacket just to make sure the derringer was still there.

Billy Joe broke the silence by saying "Mind if I smoke?"

He did not wait for my answer and had a cancer stick out and between his lips almost instantly. He fumbled a bit with a disposal lighter. It actually relaxed me a bit to see him display his own nervousness.

"What's this about, Billy Joe?" I asked.

He took a long drag on his smoke, held it in for a long couple of seconds, blew out a cloud of gray vapors that drifted up to the ceiling. We both watched the cloud for a moment then he said "Xara, my wife, Betz, is missing, and I want to hire you to find her for me."

"What do you mean missing? Where did she go? When?"

He started with a short story. It actually matched the detail of her story pretty closely. He told me the date correctly. He did leave out the part about him leaving for the office and then sneaking back into the house after Betz had left. According to his version he had said good bye to her as she left for her tennis match. He told me he was in his office where we were sitting and claimed she came back into the house but he also claimed that he never heard her coming back into the house. Then, he claimed she left the house again shortly, and he had not heard from her since. He claimed he had called the country club and found that she had cancelled her court time. He claimed he had called her cell phone several times since but he had not reached her. He claimed he had called the telephone company and according to their records her cell phone was on the network and working. He, of course, did not know for sure if it was in her possession or not. Unfortunately he claimed, but I couldn't help but think it was really fortunate for me and Betz, her cell model was rather old so it did not have a GPS which are routinely built into the newer phones.

As his tale was unfolding I caught something that I needed to question. I sort of lifted my hand feeling like a third grader in arithmetic class cautiously wishing to ask a question. He graciously paused his speech to let me ask.

"If you did not see or hear her, how do you know she came back into the house?" I queried.

"I figured you would ask that" he said.

He opened a drawer of his desk and took out two video tapes. He looked at the labels, and picked one out. He could reach out and operate the VCR by the side of his desk but I had to turn to see the image on the large television behind me. I really did not wish to have my back turned to him at the moment but it was unavoidable.

The television came to life with a low quality, grainy, black-and-white image. There was a banner along the bottom showing a date and time stamp that correctly pointed back to the date and time from the Tuesday in question. The tape clearly told me that it was January 10. It was an outside scene pointed at the driveway along the side of their house. As we were watching a car drove up. "There she comes" he said.

I watched as the car stopped and Betz, dressed in her cute little tennis outfit, hopped out of the car. She walked towards the house and just before she opened the kitchen door Billy Joe stopped it. I turned back to see what he was doing, and saw him pop the first tape out of the VCR and slide the second one in.

This tape showed the inside of the kitchen. Apparently Billy Joe took security seriously. As we were watching the door to the kitchen opened and we saw the star of the video, Betz, come into the kitchen. She paused just long enough to dump her purse and tennis equipment on the island in the middle of the room. She walked out of the room down the hall right towards us and off of camera view. The tape continued to roll for just a few seconds when we saw her enter the kitchen again, this time from the hall. She did exactly what I already knew she was going to do. She wiggled herself out of the tennis clothes, she quietly got two wine glasses out of a cupboard and placed them on the island next to her purse. She took a bottle of wine out of the refrigerator, poured a small amount into each of the two glasses, placed the opened bottle on the island next to her purse, she picked up the two wine glasses and nude with a big smile on her face she took the two wine glasses back off camera towards his office. This time she was off camera for almost a full minute. Suddenly she hurried back into the kitchen, placed the two glasses on the counter, grabbed up her purse leaving the tennis equipment where it was, fished her car keys out of her purse, headed for the door, suddenly remembered she was naked, turned around facing the camera to stoop and gather up her clothes and shoes, turned, and quietly fled the domicile.

At this point Billy Joe stopped the tape, extracted it, and shoved the first one back in. From outside the house we saw her emerge, quickly don the tennis shorts then throw the top over her head and struggle to get her arms into the sleeves. She hopped into the car and backed out at a speed way faster then the reverse gear was meant for.

Billy Joe stopped the VCR and stacked one tape on top of the other on his desk.

I started with a simple question. "Does Betz know about the security tapes?"

"What?" he questioned, obviously not understanding.

"Hey" I answered, "I really don't care where or how a married couple makes love, but it seems a little strange that she would get naked in the kitchen if she knew a camera was rolling."

"I see your point" he acquiesced. He appeared to be thinking, at least he did not answer quickly. He told me that they had installed the security system for the outside of the house three years ago right after they had bought the place. He knew for sure that she was aware of the cameras there. Then he added that only a year ago he had put a couple of cameras inside the house. He told me that he honestly could not remember ever telling Betz that the cameras inside had been installed but hadn't done anything to keep them a secrete from her. He seemed to think she couldn't have possibly lived in the house a year and not known the cameras were there. In other words he did not confirm it but he felt pretty sure she did know about the camera in the kitchen.

Of course, at the time I couldn't tell Billy Joe this but I decided to simply ask Betz if she knew she was on tape. I asked him to tell me what he thought she had been doing and what had spooked her. He put the tape of the inside shots back in the VCR. He rewound it to the spot where Betz arrived in the kitchen from outside the house. He let it run until when she first walked off camera down the hall. At that point he paused the tape and pointed out that even though we could not see her it would have put her in the hall right outside of the office we were sitting in. He also then told me that he had been, in fact, in the office at the time but claimed he had been on the phone and then he actually at this point picked up the phone and turned his chair facing away from the door to demonstrate. So according to Billy Joe's interpretation of the events Betz had seen him there and seen that he was alone so she had decided to have a little fun.

I probed "and at this point you don't know she is here in the house with you?"

"Xara" he answered, "I swear I did not hear her. She was supposed to be at a tennis game that she played every Tuesday. I had no idea she was back in the house."

At that point he pointed the remote at the VCR and rolled the tape forward. As we watched Betz undress in the kitchen Billy Joe told me that in his opinion Betz had found him in the office alone and had simply wanted to spice things up, he commented on how she was moving comfortably and freely which indicated that she was not frightened or threatened. He paused the tape as she was pulling the bottle of wine out of the refrigerator and told me all about exactly what kind of wine it had been. He made sure to tell me that they did not drink a lot and, as far as he knew, she was not in the habit of drinking in the late morning. It was almost as if he were apologizing to me that they might even consider alcohol before noon. I wish he had noticed my bourbon glass was empty because I certainly was ready for another shot.

He let the tape roll forward again and we watched Betz carry the two glasses of wine towards the office. He let the tape roll and I commented on how much longer she was off camera down the hall this time. He didn't say another word until the tape showed her hurrying back into the kitchen. He was done showing me what he wanted to show me and wanted to get on with his explanation, so he paused the tape at this point. I don't think he did it on purpose but we were left with a still picture of his lovely wife Betz in all her glory facing the camera with a look of pure terror on her face.

We both looked at the image for a few long seconds before continuing his explanation.

"Obviously" he started "she was on her way in here to be with me and something scared her. I have done my best to figure out what scared her but I just can't figure it out. As far as I can recollect I was just sitting here on the phone."

I knew he was telling the truth but at this point he did not know, at least I hoped he did not know, that I was already working for Betz, so I had to pretend I was getting this story for the first time.

"Come on Bill Joe" I said, "she came in here to jump your bones but she found you nailing some other woman."

"No!" he protested, "It couldn't have been like that. Look around this room. There is nowhere for someone else to hide. If I had been in here with another woman Betz would have seen her the first time she came down the hall while she was still dressed. If she caught me like that she never would have gone back to the kitchen, gotten naked, and then come back down the hall."

I couldn't fight his logic on that one. "What about your kids?" I asked. "Is it possible that one of them had wandered into the other end of the hall and caught her there naked?"

He looked at me like he was stunned, like he had not thought about the possibility and like he was pissed off at himself for not thinking about it. He said he would confirm where the two kids were at the time but then he told me to look at her image still on the television. "If she had caught me with another woman she would be mad. If one of my kids had seen her she would have been embarrassed. Look at her face. What do you see?"

He was right. "Terror" I whispered.

"Yes" he said.

We sat there for almost a minute before either of us said anything else.

Without asking permission I picked up our now empty glasses and crossed to the credenza to refill them. I placed the drinks on his desk and as I was sitting down I asked "And you haven't seen her or heard from her since, right?"

Billy Joe assured me he had called her cell phone several times but other than that he had not heard from her or seen her since that Tuesday and once again he made a point of telling me that he had not seen her after she had left for the tennis match but obviously she had seen him.

"And you want to hire me to track her down, right?" I continued.

"Yes" he dejectedly said. I swear to God I saw a tear roll down his cheek.

I wrestled my briefcase back into my lap and opened it up and took out a contract blank. Billy Joe had hired me before a couple of times so he was very familiar with the routine. He gave me brief answers to the questions I asked and did not argue at all about my fees. There it was, with our signatures I had officially committed the crime of double-dipping. Wait, is that a crime? Billy Joe did not even have to write me out a retainer. He had already prepared a check for ten grand to ensure my services.

As I put the contract back in my case along with the check I asked why me when he had several investigators on staff. His answer was pretty well thought out. First he said that she had probably simply left him for a younger man and he did not want one of his staffers to discover that. He also added that if she was with some other man it could even possibly be one of his staffers. I had to admit I hadn't thought of that possibility.

We spent the next twenty minutes getting data in place. I mean he gave me her schedule and all the phone numbers. He told me about her recent charity commitments. He told me which were her favorite jewelry stores. He told me her favorite ice cream, and her shoe size. He gave me her parents contact information and his as well. He cautioned me that he wanted my investigation to be as discrete as possible. I asked him what he had done about the kids, how he had explained the absence of their step mom. I mean surely they would have noticed her not being there. He told me he had told them the first day or two that she was visiting friends, but then had a frank discussion with them after the third day. He told me that he had made it clear to them that they needed to keep the story out of the papers.

I asked if he would allow me to search the house for clues and if I could look at his financial books and if I could talk to people on his staff. He told me I would have full access to anything I needed. He surprised me by even giving me a key to the house and the code to the alarm system so that I could get into the house and have access to Betz's things when I needed them even if there was nobody home. I was dying to ask about his real estate interests in Arlington but held back because my knowledge of that subject would surely tip my hand.

I had been stalling because there was something important I wanted to ask him but I could not tell him the truth and I could not think up anything very clever to bluff with, but this interview was rapidly coming to an end and it was now or never.

"Can I have those tapes?" I asked him.

"Why?" was his expected response.

"I might be able to get some sort of lead by examining the tennis outfit she was wearing. Perhaps some store clerk or gas station attendant will recognize her if he sees a picture of her in the outfit." I ambled.

"I really want this investigation handled as discreetly as possible. I do not want nude pictures of Betz all over the internet."

As he said this though he did slide the two video tapes across the desk at me. I snatched the tapes up and got them into my briefcase as quickly as possible. Now that I had them in my possession I wanted to get out of there as soon as possible. Before I could leave though he took me down the hall away from the kitchen and back into the huge entry hall. His two children had gathered in the living room and he took me in there and introduced me to them. He made sure to tell them that part of my job would be to keep the story out of the paper. He told them to expect me to be in the house whenever I wanted to be, and he also told them to cooperate with me and tell me the absolute truth whenever I asked them a question. They both agreed to help in any way they could. The son seemed a bit more sincere though when he was promising then the daughter did.

Walking from the door to my car I realized that I was not quite as frightened as I had been walking up to the door. I mean I had actually believed most of what he had told me. He really seemed sincere in his motive for wanting to find Betz. Was I missing something? Could he be the wronged person here? I told myself that just because I had heard Betz's version of the story first, and just because she had hired me first, that didn't make her version of the story any more likely to be true than his version. Two things though popped into my mind. The first was the look of terror on Betz's face that Billy Joe and I had both clearly seen. The other was the proof I already had that Billy Joe was in the habit of sneaking into his own house when his wife was out at her tennis dates.

It was almost nine o'clock by the time I was safely back at my office/home. I took off the leather jacket and hung it on a coat tree we have in the corner near the front door. I put the tapes in my little safe. It was not a big security safe to keep burglars away from my goodies. It was a little metal box that was supposed to keep the contents safe in case of flood or fire. I did not know how good it really was because it had never been in either a fire or flood since I had bought it, but it was there for exactly the purpose of protecting important information so that is where I put the tapes.

I was really hungry so I investigated my own kitchen. My super sleuthing powers led me to the conclusion that it was time to go shopping. Apparently I had stocked the kitchen of the rental where I had stashed my client better than I had stocked my own. I did find a can of tomato soup and a box of crackers so I could push the shopping trip off until tomorrow. In ten minutes I was seated at my desk with a big bowl of soup and a can of diet Coke. I had flipped on the radio and it was stuck on an oldies station that played a lot of rock and roll music from the year I had graduated high-school. Perfect. The soup was delicious and with my tummy no longer growling at me I started feeling a little better. I shoved the empty soup bowl to one side and put my brief case on my desk. As I opened it I realized it still held my colt and I was, in fact, still quite well armed.

I took the colt and put it away in the safe next to the tapes. I took the pepper spray out of my back pocket and dropped it into a device many women accessorize with all the time but I myself seem to rarely find a reason to carry called a purse. I went to the coat tree and retrieved the derringer from the pocket of my jacket and shoved it into the top right drawer of my desk. I tried to extract the knife from inside my pant leg where I had taped it and found I could not easily get it out of it's hiding hole. Not my best idea I guess. I mean if I could not extract the weapon here in the safety and privacy of my own home how would I have been expected to use it in battle? I made sure the front door was locked and shucked the jeans off. I turned them inside out and pulled the tape off of the switchblade. Once the switchblade was safely stashed and clad now in t-shirt and panties I sat at my desk and started working on my notes from this days activities. That is where Laura found me when she walked through the front door five hours later.

CHAPTER-06.

I had a dilemma. I had accepted the job working for Billy Joe Jenton because I thought it would give me a good reason to get inside and look for clues which should make my real job, of proving he was trying to kill his wife, a lot easier. Morally, the sooner I got to the bottom of the mystery the safer my real client, Betz, would be. Of course I also took the job because I was afraid that if I didn't take the job Billy Joe might figure out that I was already working for Betz and he might then decide to do something to get me out of the way. In other words I was scared of the man. I had been armed, but on his home turf he could have had a cannon under his desk pointing right at me the whole time and I wouldn't have even known it. Yes, I had been terrified, but that, in itself, was not a good reason to sign on with Billy Joe when I was supposed to be working for Betz.

I really wanted to go right over to the rental and tell Betz exactly what had happened and spin it as if I were doing it on purpose as if it were a common investigative technique. I couldn't do that though because I didn't know how much truth I was getting from her, and besides, Billy Joe had seemed very sincere about finding her for all the right reasons. I knew someone was hosing me but at this point it might be Billy Joe, or Betz, or even worse both of them. So I couldn't come clean with her, at least not yet. I needed to talk with someone. I had a little secrete and I just had to share it with someone. Laura was out of the question. I mean I really didn't want to involve her in something that had all the ear marks of a really dangerous situation. I knew hundreds of people but none of them well enough that I could count on them keeping a secret. I guess I wouldn't make much of a gossip.

I thought of talking with Mandy but she was totally uncontrollable. I mean she enjoyed my friendship and probably realized that I was only friendly with her when I needed her help, but she was so easily bought I could practically count on the opposition exploiting her as easily as I had. It did not matter that the opposition was at this time unidentified.

I also considered discussing the matter with Dutch or AJ but an accidental slip in front of Betz would be a disaster. Normally they would have been the first people I would have confided in but unfortunately I had already committed them to a role in this drama.

Well this was Friday morning, and it was time to get busy. I had three things I wanted to accomplish this day.

The most important was to get into Billy Joe's house and look around a bit. I really wanted to do it when he was not at home, and it would also be nice if the kids were not there. I would need to interview them eventually but I wanted to snoop first. The things I found while carefully examining their private spaces might generate many questions I would need to ask them that I wouldn't even know about before I snooped. Even if I had to do it in plain view of the whole family I would still have to get over there and look thru Betz's clothes and such. The best I could do right now was predict when they might all be out of the house and take my chances. I would, though, have to have a cover story ready in case Billy Joe was there.

The second agenda item for today was to get the results of the background searches on the four men that were on the short list of who Billy Joe was talking with when Betz had caught him in the office. The results would be posted in my e-mail box by now and I was confident I would get a good lead or two from them, but I could not get my hopes up too much for what I might find there. Besides, no matter how bad the reports said the fellows were I still would not know which one Betz had overheard. Still, getting the reports and looking them over would be an important part of my days work. Depending on what I found there I might have to add a lot of immediate follow-up work.

The third thing to accomplish today was that I wanted to take a good close look at the video tapes I had of Betz. There was something very specific I wanted to see from the tape that would help a lot. The tape had a date and time stamp on it but those were traditionally very unreliable. The reason you can't count on them is that they are usually set to the correct time when the system is first installed but then nobody ever makes corrections over time. For instance if the clock in the camera looses just one minute each month then the time stamp will be wrong by twelve minutes after a year. I needed the exact time that the video was shot. According to the telephone luds Billy Joe had made four calls all within eleven minutes. Betz had overheard Billy Joe make his threat during one of those calls. If I could narrow down the exact time the video was shot then I could narrow down which phone call. My hope was that the camera would pick up all the action we had already seen but that it also would possibly be pointed at some clock in the background. If there were a clock on the wall in the kitchen that was on camera I could use that time to pinpoint which call Billy Joe was on when Betz walked down that hall.

I put the tape in my own VCR and watched it. I did not see a big old clock in the background. The quality of the video was not good but I knew it could be enhanced through technology. I had neither the equipment or the knowledge needed for the job but I knew someone who did.

I wrote out a note detailing exactly what I had planned and dated it and signed it and left it in my top desk drawer. I did not expect Laura or anyone else to find the note during the day, but if my chopped up body parts were found in an old oil drum then the investigators of the crime would probably look through my desk.

At nine-thirty I dialed the number for the guard at the rental. I did not know if it would be Bear or Tiger but I had arranged it so that they traded off a cell phone when they traded shifts so that I could always get in touch with whichever one was on duty with a single number. The guard told me that everything was just fine and all was secure. The lovely Betz had stayed up late last night drinking wine and watching videos from the local rental store so she was still asleep. He had no idea what she had planned for the day but assured me that he would keep her safe. I promised to come by later in the day.

I gathered up my forensic equipment which wasn't near as impressive as the kits hauled around on those crime scene investigation television shows. Basically I use a flash-light and a smaller version of the magnifying glass seen often by my idol, Sherlock

Holmes. I also have a set of lock picks but I am not very good at using them and I had a key to Billy Joe's house so I left the picks in my desk for this trip. I have one other very important piece of equipment that I use for forensics; a digital camera. When I bought the model it was for sure the most expensive piece of equipment I had ever bought. I got the very best model they made at the time and also bought several memory sticks for it and extra rechargeable batteries. All of this equipment fit nicely into a little leather pouch that I carried like a purse but could even be hooked onto my belt when I needed my hands free.

I wasn't sure what the day might bring, so I stashed the two video tapes of Betz in the trunk of my Taurus and pointed it towards the Jenton home. I parked where I had the night before and rang the door bell. I waited nervously on the front porch for three minutes and finally realized that my luck had turned good. Nobody was home. I slipped the key into the lock, turned it, opened the door, and hurried over to the beeping alarm where I entered the disarming code.

I had the house to myself but I did not know for how long so I moved quickly. I wanted to examine Billy Joe's office while he was absent so that should have been first on my list but there was actually one room that was even more important right at the moment. I headed to the kitchen, located the camera, and stood right near it looking out trying to get a camera-eye view of the area. It was about then that I realized that any thing I did in the house was likely to be captured on tape so Billy Joe could watch me at his leisure later on. I also thought about this and realized that I didn't know the number or location of other cameras. Well, on-camera or not, I still had to process the house while I could.

Looking over the kitchen from where the camera sat I saw two clocks that interested me. The first was the clock display on the microwave. It glowed red and according to my watch it was set to the correct time. The only problem was that it faced a direction that made it improbable that the camera had captured it. The other was a wall clock over the sink but the clock currently showed noon straight up and the second hand was not moving. Oh well. I mentally noted the location of the clocks but did not take any pictures of them. Not really expecting to find anything important but because I knew I was on camera in this room I carefully opened every drawer and every cabinet door peering inside and occasionally picking up an item and closely examining it before replacing it. I even looked in the fridge and opened the oven.

Done with the kitchen I walked down the hall towards Billy Joe's office. I was pretty confident that there was no camera in the office. First of all I just didn't think Billy Joe would want his every move taped, and secondly if there were a tape of him alone and on the phone while Betz snuck up to him and then fled I am sure he would have showed me that tape as well. I felt comfortable in my privacy at the moment but went quickly to work. There was something that bothered me about the video I had seen that I wanted to check out. I could understand Billy Joe not seeing Betz when she came in but why didn't he hear her? I will admit that if he was concentrating on the phone call he happened to be engaged in at the time, he may not have heard her walking around in the kitchen, but when she was standing either just outside his office door or even maybe just inside the door, he probably would have heard her foot steps. As I walked slowly down the hall I noticed a very plush carpeting on the floor. I was as quiet as I possibly could be and listened intently. I did not hear my own foot steps.

Standing at the door way I took a few quick shots with my digital just to map the entire room. I sat in his desk chair and went through the desk. I found much what I expected to find and not much else. I did not turn his computer on but I did take a picture of it so that I could record the make and model. This would become important later in the day. I picked up the phone. I did not dial anyone but I pretended I was on the phone. I tried turning the chair back and forth and had to admit that the most comfortable position was, in fact, with the chair turned so that my back was to the door that Betz would have entered. Sitting as I was I saw that there was a window in my view but I could not see a reflection in it in which I might monitor the door even though I was facing away from it.

There were two file cabinets in the office. I opened the first and found it to be regular files in manila folders arranged alphabetically. I did not go through the files in detail but I did open each drawer as far as I could and took several pics of each drawer hopefully recording the labels on the files. The second cabinet was most interesting of all. It had four drawers and each drawer held forty video tapes. The top drawer was labeled "North", the second was labeled "South", the third was labeled "Entry", and the fourth drawer was called "Kitchen". Based simply on the drawer labels I could now deduce that there were a total of four video cameras each hooked up to it's own VCR. This was a simple system that had been put together one piece at a time. If it had been a sophisticated complex system there would have been a single VCR recording all four cameras at the same time controlled by a computer that split the signals and combined them in such a way that you could store or play back the single tape and see all four views. Seeing the four separate tapes I expected that Billy Joe had set up the outside surveillance first with one camera capturing the house from the perspective of the front door which was on the north side of the house and the other one pointed at the rear entrance, the one by the kitchen, which door, of course, is at the south side of the house.

When these two cameras were installed the company designing the system would have spoken with Billy Joe about it. They would have put some money into the cameras that would make them motion sensitive so that they did not record hours and hours of nothing happening but only things where something was moving about. That way a single two-hour tape could be used to capture up to a weeks worth of traffic depending on how much activity there was in the area. Once they had the sophisticated cameras set up they had to choose which VCRs to use. The complex machines that allowed multiple input and could record several cameras at the same time cost about ten times as much as the regular household VCR machine that could record just the one camera. Still, if you just had a couple of cameras it was a lot cheaper to buy multiple VCRs then to buy one complex unit. Further, I could deduce that the drawer labeled "Entry" probably was installed later and probably shot the front door and entry way from the inside of the house. Finally I expected the camera in the kitchen had been installed last simply to capture the folks coming in the back door. Billy Joe had told me as much but it was nice to see his words confirmed.

I looked carefully in the drawer labeled "South". All of the tapes were stacked in order of date with the labels easily read as you were looking into the drawer. There were forty slots in the drawer and there were two empty slots. One slot that was empty was the one where someone, Billy Joe probably, had removed the oldest tape and relabeled it and stuck it in the VCR to record today's events. The other empty slot was for the tape that would have been for January 10, which was the tape Billy Joe had given me. To me this indicated that he had simply pulled the tape out of the drawer and handed it to me. If he had made a copy he probably would have filed the copy back in the drawer here where it belonged.

The drawer with the tapes from the kitchen camera also had two empty slots whose dates exactly correlated with the two dates, one for today and one for the date in question. Not surprisingly the other two drawers were full except for the empty slots representing today's tapes. Well, O.K. I had found the tapes, the VCRs couldn't be far away. To change the tapes on a daily basis would become a chore so Billy Joe would want the daily task to be as effortless as possible, therefore I thought the VCRs must be somewhere here in this room. I looked around and saw a door that I expected was a closet. It was. I took a couple of shots of the closet with my digital but there was nothing there other than what I had expected. A shelving unit had been built into the closet and it currently held four industrial looking VCRs. All four had glowing indicator lights proving that they were on. There was a hole in the ceiling of the closet that let in a fat bunch of wires that ran to the machines. On the lower shelves I found several six-packs of new tapes to be used. There were also some other office supply stuff there like boxes of replacement staples for his desk top stapler, unopened reams of paper both plain and with his letterhead, a short stack of four or five unused legal pads, a bucket with a couple of hundred loose pens and pencils. Nothing important or unexpected at all. No bag of unreported cash, no stash of party drugs, no video tapes labeled "Betz Does Dallas" or "Billy Joe and the Cheerleaders", no empty bourbon bottles, no spent condoms.

On the other side of the first floor one entered from the entry hall past the stair case into a formal living room. Beyond that were several other rooms all dedicated to family living. The formal living room looked beautiful but completely untouched by human hands. The family room had a big plasma television with wires sticking in the back and also coming out the front of the system. They had three of the most popular game playing machines and a big stack of DVD type games to play on them. Not too surprising for a house with two wealthy teens. There was a nice leather couch and three good recliners. The coffee table held four game controllers and a half dozen remote controls. It also had several rings on it's surface where a Coke can had been left a little too long. There was a small table in one corner with a telephone on it. Pillows were scattered on the floor near the phone table and near the table stacked along one wall I found dozens of fashion magazines. The phone looked well used but endearingly there was on the table a brand new note pad and gold Cross pen for taking messages. The note pad and pen both had a cover of dust on them and it was blatantly obvious that no messages had ever been written down there. I could just see the daughter Adrian sitting on the pillows flipping through one of the magazines talking on the phone with a girl friend while her brother Bubby and two or three of his friends played Doom or Grand Theft Auto or the current version of Madden.

A door to the left yielded to a study with one complete wall of book shelves which was slowly loosing the battle and currently storing more movie videos than actual books. There were two matching small desks where the kids were probably supposed to do their homework. Both had that same thin cover of dust from disuse. The desk drawers revealed little that would help me solve this mystery but I did photograph everything and snatched a couple of scribbled notes so I would have a sample of each of the kids writing. I did not expect I would ever need these but who knew what the future of this case might bring. Hey, I half expected a kidnap ransom note to mysteriously appear any time now and having the kids writing samples would help me eliminate them.

Back in the family room the door to the right yielded a small but nice bathroom. I think it is a blonde thing but whenever I see a bathroom I immediately need one so I closed the door and squatted praying that if anyone walked into the house while I was snooping that they would not pick this exact moment. The medicine cabinet was bare except for aspirin and first aide supplies, mostly unopened.

I wondered where the family ate their meals. I headed back to the kitchen and there, right where you would expect it, was the doorway to the large dining room. It, in turn led back to the grand entry way. The dining room was nice and I captured it on my camera, but it too yielded nothing of current significance.

I was feeling a bit frustrated. I mean I had searched the entire first floor and found exactly zilch. On the other hand my luck was still holding as I was still the only person in the abode. I walked up the marbled stair case feeling a lot like Scarlet O'Hara in Gone With The Wind. Upstairs I found five nice bed rooms and three bath rooms. Two bedrooms were set up as guest bed rooms and gave me no new clues to investigate. The dressers and closets were completely empty, the furniture polished.

I found first Adrian's room. Clothes! Clothes stuffed into and overflowing the closet, clothes jammed into every drawer of two good sized dressers, clothes tossed and stacked on two chairs, clothes strewn all over the bed, a ton of clothing hiding the carpeting. A jewelry box that was nearly as large as my desk that had a collection of semi-precious ornaments that had this girl quite jealous. A Chinese puzzle box that I quickly opened and found two tabs of what was probably X. Nothing on the walls except a single poster and it said a lot. It was an old black and white blow-up of that famous old poster of John Lennon and Yoko Ono standing there in their birthday suits. Why in this new millennium would a sixteen year-old girl have just one poster? Why would it be this poster? What parents allowed a teen-ager to hang nude posters even if it was of John and Yoko?

Bubby's room revealed mostly what I would expect from a fourteen year old boy. Surprisingly it was much cleaner than the girls room but it still had a bit of lived in messiness. He was somewhere between little boy and full grown man. His walls were completely covered mostly with sports heroes and rock stars. The older male rock star posters currently being covered over by fresh young female rockers in skimpy stage costumes. His desk had a new looking computer which I did not attempt to turn on but I did photograph it as I had his father's computer. There were science books in a book case. I found a stash of Playboys under the bed. I found a stash of junk food in the drawer of the bedside table.

Finally it was onto the master bedroom where the happy couple shared their conjugal bliss. It was as large as the floor plan of my entire house. I was quite careful in this room. I did not immediately take any pictures. Even though I had discovered the obvious video cameras, I felt that if Billy Joe's reputation was even half true, it would not be impossible for him to have a camera set up in this room as well. Eventually I did find it. The room had a large bed dominating the center of the room splitting it into two separate zones. It was easy to determine which side of the room was his and which was hers. In Billy Joe's defense he seemed to yield the more spacious chunk of bedroom to Betz. There was a large closet on each side of the room. Both closets had double sliding doors which were completely covered by mirrors. This gave the room a never-ending illusion. You could easily walk into her closet and it was well appointed with dressers and cupboards and hanging space. It would take me a week to thoroughly go over the closet in detail. I couldn't afford the time right now so I flashed several pics and crossed to the masculine side of the room.

Behind Billy Joe's mirrored closet doors I found what I had been looking for. The closet was nowhere near as large as Betz's closet but still fairly large. It was neatly stuffed with thousand dollar suits but there also is where I found another camera with it's own video recorder. I stepped into the closet and found that one of the mirrored doors was one way glass so that from inside the closet one could easily see the bed and any activity on it. The camera, of course, was pointed in that direction, but, thankfully, it was currently turned off. Scattered on the floor were dozens of unlabeled video tapes. I went over to the bed and on Billy Joe's bedside table I found the remote that would turn the camera on and off. I quickly went to the side of the room that faced the front of the house and looked around. I could clearly see the driveway and so far my car was still the only one there. I ran back to Billy Joe's closet and picked two of the tapes at random from the mess on the floor.

Since I had no purse with me I had to carry the videos in plain sight so I hustled my ass down the stairs, set the alarm, got out the door, locked it, and made it to my car before anyone saw me. I was half-way home when I realized that my exit was probably taped by the north camera. All I could do at this time was pray that Billy Joe would not notice the videos I was carrying.

It was one P.M. and I had knocked the most important thing off my to-do list. The next most important thing would be to talk to AJ's husband, Dutch, but he wouldn't be home from work for another five hours. I thought about going by the rental and giving Betz an update, but since I wanted to see Dutch in person I could do that later when I went to see him. I headed back to the house/office and sat down at my desk. I was oh so tempted to take a sneak peek at the videos I had pilfered from Billy Joe's closet but a more important item at this time was to read the results of the four background checks I had done. I should have figured it was wasting time because I really felt that we could narrow the time frame down a little better, but that couldn't be done without help and right now I was flying solo.

I fired up the old computer and logged onto my business e-mail address. There were eleven new messages in my in-box. Seven of them I deleted immediately because I am very happy with the current size of my penis and really do not need any small blue pills that promise to make me stallion-like. That left four e-mails and two were solicitations to join a travel discount service. I mean they were two identical messages sent two days apart. They went directly into my trash bin and I made a vow to rework the thingy that filtered out the junk mail. Of the two e-mails that were actually important to me one was correspondence from a previous client that sounded like they needed my help again, and the response I was looking for with the background checks.

I stored the message from the potential repeat client. Business was suddenly looking better and better.

Finally I clicked the open button of the message I had waited for. Betz had told me that she had gotten a call from her friend to cancel the tennis match around 9:45. When someone tells me that the time was "around" 9:45, I usually figure it was somewhere between 9:30 and 10:00 leaving about fifteen minutes either way. I needed to work with the widest parameters. If she had heard from her friend at 9:30 and she had immediately marched down to the pro shop to cancel her court time and then had immediately hopped into her car and driven the two miles from the club to their house, and had immediately entered the kitchen upon her arrival, then she could have been back to the house by about 9:56 or 9:57. On the other hand, if her friend had called at 10:00, and they had chatted for two or three minutes, and she had gone to the pro shop and immediately canceled her court time but then tried on two tennis outfits she might be considering buying, and then had run into a friend in the parking lot and chatted for a few minutes and then encountered heavier than expected traffic on her way home she could have walked into the house as late as about 10:35-10:40. Regardless of what the time-stamp on the VCR tape said, I would have to check out all of the calls Billy Joe had made or received from 9:55 through 10:41. Fortunately for me the luds that Mandy had provided showed that neither the land line or Billy Joe's cell had received any calls during that time frame. As I mentioned earlier though the land line had been used to make four outgoing calls during that time frame. My investigative efforts had yielded up the owners of the numbers that the land line had called during that time period and now I was about to get some background information on the four suspects. Unfortunately, all I had was the time and duration of the calls, I did not have recordings of the actual phone calls. I had to keep in mind that the actual owner of the phone that Billy Joe was calling would not necessarily be the person who answered the call.

The actual e-mail showed me how much they were billing me and a copy of the request I had made to them. It was then filled with information about how to take advantage of all of the services they offered in the future for all my background check needs. Down at the bottom there were four separate attachments. I downloaded the attachments without reading them making them permanent members of my hard drive to do with as I may want until such a time as they were no longer valuable to me. After the electronic magic of downloading completed in just a few moments I logged off of my mail account and off the internet so I had the computer with it's four new reports all to myself. I clicked on the four new icons one at a time and again without reading a thing hit the print button. One of the really cool things about computers, at least from my point of view, is that the reports were printed off but were still on my hard drive so I could be reckless and carefree with the paperwork and if I completely destroyed it I could simply print it off again. I mean I didn't even have to be careless. I could even be simply frivolous and do something like print the reports on light blue paper only because I did not like the look of white paper at the time. I felt ever so powerful.

I gathered up the papers and made sure I had all that I needed and separated them into the four reports they were and stapled together each report. In total I had about twenty pieces of paper to get through.

Billy Joe had made a call at 10:01 that lasted four minutes. The number he called had been owned by a Mr. Stanley Rand. I placed the name "Stanley Rand" at the head of a new sheet on my steno pad and dutifully added his address which was in Dallas. As I read his report I took other notes that might be helpful but at this point I had no idea what I was actually looking for. Mr. Rand worked for a delivery service and had no criminal record at all. His employment record made him sound like the kind that hopped from one company to another often but always worked for some company where the pick-up truck he owned was a greater value to his employer than he actually was.

Immediately following that call at 10:05 Billy Joe had dialed Mr. Jeff Watley of Irving, Texas. That call had lasted until 10:12. I gave Mr. Watley his own page in my steno book. This call could have been a real possibility time wise. Mr. Watley was a Real Estate Agent that worked for a local Realtor. He had graduated from Texas Christian University in Fort Worth five years ago and had been arrested twice since then. Both arrests had been for burglary and neither had gone to court so as far as the official word would be his record was clean because he had never been proven guilty in a court of law, but, for some reason, at least twice in the last couple of years, the cops had hauled him in, questioned him about a recent crime, charged him, but then not been able to get him past a grand jury. He had been born local, he had grown up local, he had gone to college just 20 miles from Irving, he currently lived in Irving, and he was employed selling Irving real estate. I am sure he did not grow up as Billy Joe's best friend because he was more than a decade younger, but he certainly could be well known to the Jenton clan.

After that call Billy Joe had been off the phone for seven minutes, and then at 10:19 he called Mr. Travis Solter. Travis Solter was an attorney from New Orleans. When hurricane Katrina had hit in 2005 he had, like so many others from the gulf coast, found himself homeless. Fortunately Travis had been able to gather his wife and two kids together and actually drive his own car out of the New Orleans area. Their house was completely destroyed and the law firm he worked for was pretty much wiped out. They had come to the Dallas area only because so many others were heading for Houston. He had an impressive background as far as education and employment. He worked in the same industry Billy Joe did but not for the same law firm. He and his wife had rented a house in Irving when they first arrived but the report said the lease was up a month ago and had no data about where they lived now. It was, of course, possible that they had simply extended the lease. Billy Joe had spoken with Mr. Solter until 10:30.

Almost immediately after that Billy Joe had dialed up Aaron Wilson, also of Irving, Texas. The conversation had lasted only a single minute. Still it could have been the magic minute in which Betz had overheard Billy Joe say the incriminating words. Aaron had little in his background of interest. He lived here in town but had drifted here about the same time Billy Joe and Betz had gotten married. He had never been arrested. He had been in the army before moving to Irving. His background check said nothing about college and he currently worked for a lawn care service. I fully expected Billy Joe was just scheduling his lawn's next clipping, which is something we do year round in Texas.

Well now I had the names and backgrounds of my four prime suspects. Of course I still did not know what they were actually suspects for. So far they were simply being suspected of being on the phone with Billy Joe when his wife happened to get a little frisky on a Tuesday morning. I looked the list of four names over. I would set up a ruse. I made a list of the four names, then added four names from actual people who lived in the Irving area and whom I was reasonably certain that Betz would recognize, but whom I was quite sure had nothing at all to do with the case. To that I added four more names all of which I just made up on the spot. That left me with a list of twelve names. I would alphabetize the twelve names and present them to Betz to see which she admitted knowing. Her knowledge of the people would prove nothing, but if she claimed to know the names I had made up, or claimed she did not know the names of the four I had added, then it would prove she was lying to me. If she told me the truth, and if she actually did know any of the suspects she might be able to help me understand what their connection to Billy Joe was.

It was three o'clock in the afternoon on a Friday. I had heard Laura's alarm go off so I knew she would be up soon. I quickly headed for the kitchen to start a fresh pot of coffee. It was still too early to head over to the rental and I really didn't have anything else I needed to accomplish before then so I pulled out the two videos I had pilfered from Billy Joe's closet floor. I felt guilty for just a moment because I knew Laura would come out to see me soon and I didn't want her seeing my client/suspect on tape doing who knows what, but what the heck, she was a big girl. I popped the first tape into our VCR. Immediately the TV was filled with naked bodies. It was definitely the bedroom I had just snooped through. There were two bodies on the bed. One was Billy Joe and the other was a woman I did not recognize. The tape rolled on displaying their lust for just a minute or two then went blank for a second. When the picture came back it was Billy Joe and another woman. As the scene with the second woman ended the tape again went blank and then started a third mini-affair. Laura walked into the room with a cup of coffee during the third tryst so I paused the action and explained briefly what I was watching. She pulled up a chair to join in the fun.

Since I was just a few minutes into the tape I rewound it so Laura would be able to see the opening credits. The tape lasted less than an hour when we just let it play through. All together we counted fourteen women and always Billy Joe. It was Laura who pointed out that you could see Billy Joe operating the camera's remote control while the action was going on. I did not recognize any of the women but Laura thought she recognized two of them as her co-workers. With that many women one would think there would be a lot of kinks but there weren't. No bondage, never more than just two in the bed at any one time. Billy Joe seemed to prefer to be laying on his back with his bed-mate sitting on top of him. Laura pointed out that it might just be that it would have been hard to operate the remote if he had been on top, so it might just mean that he didn't record everything. There was a good deal of oral sex with Billy Joe seeming to prefer giving rather than getting. None of the girls seemed to object to this. All in all it was quite boring to watch.

The women themselves were a mixture. Some white, some black, a couple of Hispanics, one Asian.

All were pretty but none really were drop dead gorgeous. All were young and healthy looking. Something really bothered me about this tape. I couldn't bring it to the surface. I mean there were dozens of tapes on Billy Joe's closet floor and this one had more than a dozen different ladies on it but none of the ladies was there more than once. Also, each appeared on tape for just a brief period of time. Further more why would someone be so interested that they would capture their own sex acts on tape but have no super kinky action. I mean wouldn't you film the really memorable good stuff. This tape all showed plenty of young naked flesh doing the nasty but it was far from the hottest action one could purchase at any adult video store. To me it just didn't look like a tape one would play back and fondly watch while masturbating. It didn't feel like a Hustler magazine, it had more the feel of a Victoria's Secrets catalogue.

I would have to take a much more careful look at the tape and make copious notes, and try to figure out when the sex romps had happened. Billy Joe, or whoever had set up the camera, had set it to record without that banner at the bottom showing date and time. I would have to catalogue everything, and probably try to find out who the young starlets were maybe even interviewing the two Laura recognized. For sure if I were simply doing divorce work I would have all the evidence I needed. I knew this case was about protection and attempted murder, not divorce, but this tape might prove to be very valuable if divorce ever came into play, and there were dozens of other tapes still on the floor of his closet where I had gotten this one.

Right now though I had just an hour before I wanted to leave for the rental and my important meeting with Dutch, so instead of detailing slowly through the first video Laura and I popped in the second tape expecting much the same. We did not get what we expected. This tape featured my two clients. Billy Joe was the male lead in this drama and his co-star was the lovely Betz. Whoever was in charge of costumes must not have had much of a budget because neither actor ever wore anything but their skin. Her actions were the primary subject matter for this documentary. Some of the action was sex but again it was not very kinky or edgy. I am sure some of the sex acts would make my mother blush but all of them would be considered normal play for a happily married heterosexual couple. Sex though was not the only thing on the tape. Nude we watched Betz dance for her husband. Nude we saw her best Jane Fonda workout however we did not see the tape she must have been watching. There was no sound so the dancing and workout seemed foolish but it was easy to imagine some soft music playing in the background. Nude but with actual pompoms in her hands we saw Betz cheer for an imaginary sports team. Nude we saw Betz sit on the bed, pick three penis shaped battery operated toys from a collection of dozens. Nude we saw her fill three of her orifices with the three she had picked. Nude we saw Billy Joe with a big smile on his face while he was watching, his smile not being the only part that was noticeably big.

This tape lasted forty-seven minutes. Laura had to hurriedly scoot out the door and head off to work as it finished. I really did not know what to do with my new sex videos. I mean neither really helped in my current case. The first proved that Billy Joe was a cheater but we already knew that. The second proved that there was little Betz Jenton would not do to please her husband no matter how degrading, but she had told me as much several times now. The tapes had been casually scattered in Billy Joe's closet so there was absolutely no reason for me to believe that Betz was unaware of the camera. It also proved that Billy Joe did not mind if Betz knew he was cheating. She could gather up that evidence any time she wished simply by picking up the videos from the closet and presenting them to a divorce judge. Something more was going on here and I wanted to get to the bottom of it.

The two cassettes were unlabeled and I wanted to write something on them so I could distinguish which was which. Labeling someone else's sex videos though was difficult. I just couldn't think of anything to write on the labels. Finally I scratched the word "Betz" on the one she was the star of, and "Others" on the other tape. Give me an A+ for originality. I placed the sex tapes in the safe and took out the two surveillance tapes.

Finally it was time to head to Arlington. I printed off the pictures I had taken of Billy Joe's computer and also his son's computer and put the prints in my briefcase. I loaded the two surveillance reels into my brief case and fired up the Taurus. I parked in AJ's driveway and went first to their door. My timing had been about perfect as Dutch had gotten home from work just minutes ago. I had been waiting for this meeting all day. Dutch was very important to the next phase of my investigation. I asked him if we might have a chat in his office and we closed the door leaving AJ to wonder what was going on. Dutch is a self-taught techno-wizard. He has a top of the line computer system that he is constantly upgrading. Additionally he has every device ever manufactured to hook up to a computer and some that he has just sort of figured out himself and sort of invented. He knew more about computer hardware than most engineers and could out code just about anyone in any computer language plus he had all the packaged software you could possibly get to make everything work. His office was a real mess of wires and connectors and little black boxes. Strewn all over the tops of things everywhere were software CDs and diskettes many without any labels but all right where Dutch knew they were. I was lost and intimidated by the room itself fearing I would break something just by touching it or asking it's purpose.

Dutch pushed some software packages and tech magazines off a chair and offered it to me. Gingerly I sat keeping my briefcase on my lap and my elbows close to my body for fear of bumping into a cable that might be carrying a death threat worth of juice at the time.

First I took out the pictures of the two computers I had seen in the Jenton home. I asked Dutch what the easiest way would be to get all the data off the hard drives without disturbing anything. He looked on an internet search thing identifying the computers so he could figure out how large the two hard drives probably were. Then he pulled out a little device and showed me how to hook it up. Basically the device is a removable hard-drive harness which plugs into a USB port that I didn't really know what was but Dutch showed me. I would have to go to the computer store and buy a big ass hard drive to load into the device but then I could just plug it into their computers and copy the whole hard drive. Unfortunately Dutch estimated though that the copy time would be about an hour for each computer.

I took out the two video tapes and explained really briefly what they were and what I wanted to find from them. He stood up from his own chair and walked across the office. He had to physically pull a shelving unit a little closer to the center of his office to get to a closet door. I did not even know the closet was there and I had been in this office dozens of times before. The closet was lined with shelves and the shelves were crammed with more tech hardware and old computer parts. He came back with a small device which could play a VCR tape into his computer. Easily he shoved the massive shelving unit back in front of the door.

Dutch somehow found the right little black box and proper wires so the tape player was quickly hooked up to his computer. I handed him the first tape and soon we saw Betz, in grainy black and white get out of her car at the south entrance of the Jenton Home. Dutch would be hard at work now for a long time doing what he loves to do so I made an excuse to leave the room, but not before swearing him to secrecy and making sure to tell him that Betz could not see the tapes or even hear of their existence. I realized that Betz did know the tapes existed, but I did not want Dutch showing them to her and this little white lie seemed at the time the best way to ensure that.

AJ was cooking in her own kitchen but it was ever so obvious that she was cooking way more than what she and Dutch could consume. I immediately felt a little guilty because I had just sent Dutch off on a hunt when AJ was obviously expecting dinner guests. It was, after all a Friday night, and they did, of course, have a social life that did not revolve around me. She quickly put me at ease though by telling me that Betz and Tiger were at the video rental store and would be coming by for dinner in half an hour. She also insisted that I stay for the banquette. Cool. AJ and I had a nice friendly chat avoiding all reference to the case while I sat on a stool at her breakfast bar and watched this amazing and giving woman lovingly wash carrots and slice them into bite sized bits. The cooking lesson went on as the wonderful aroma of roasted chicken as well as freshly baking bread filled the kitchen and I closely observed. All the while a steady stream of gossip poured forth from her covering all topics from current world events to our mutual friends and ending with the latest scandal on her favorite televisions show, American Idol.

When Betz and Tiger arrived AJ told me it would be about thirty minutes until dinner was ready so I took the opportunity to catch up with both Betz and Tiger. Tiger gave me a brief rundown of their activities over the past two days actually referring to a small note pad a couple of times so that he could include events that happened under Bear's guard rather than his own. There was nothing there. They were not spending every minute safely hiding in the rental, but their out-of-house choices seemed appropriately cautious.

I did not tell Betz, or anyone else for that matter, that Billy Joe had hired me, but I did tell her I had figured out a safe way I could get into her house and asked if there was anything there she needed I might fetch for her. She thought about it a bit but couldn't come up with anything. She did ask about the kids and I gave her a brief update about them. She claimed to miss them terribly but did not, for instance, request that I contact them for her and give them a secrete message about her safety. I took the opportunity to pull out my list of twelve names. First I handed it to Betz with a pen and told her to ask no questions at all but to go over the list and cross off all the names she did not know and had never heard before.

She took the pen and the list and studied the list for a good couple of minutes before making any marks with the pen. Eventually she handed it back to me.   At first glance I saw she had passed the truthfulness test by crossing off all four of the fictitious names I had added to the list and leaving alone the four names that had nothing to do with the case but were names I thought she would know. Of the four important names on the list the only one she crossed off was Stanley Rand the pick-up truck driver.

One at a time we went over the names still on the list with me asking her where she knew them from and how well she knew them. I included all seven of the names left on the list because I did not want her to know I had tested her.

About Aaron Wilson; she said he was their regular lawn care man and had been providing lawn care in the neighborhood before they had moved in. He had come highly recommended by the neighbors and they had hired him shortly after moving to the house. She claimed that the last time she had actually talked to him was a week before Thanksgiving because she had thrown a neighborhood party the Saturday after Thanksgiving and had hired him to act as valet which he had done. She had the Saturday before Thanksgiving talked to him to ask him to do the valet work and had also talked to him the evening of the party when he arrived and also when she paid him as he left late that night.

About Travis Solter; she told me he was a lawyer that Billy Joe hung out with and talked to often. She knew his wife and had attended a few functions where she had been the bauble on Travis's arm while Betz was performing the same duties for Billy Joe. She did say that both Travis and his wife had been invited to the party after Thanksgiving but that Travis had attended alone.

When speaking about Jeff Watley there was a noticeable tremor in her voice. At first she started saying that he was a fairly new acquaintance that was a real estate agent that Billy Joe was working with on the new stadium project in Arlington. She began telling me that Billy Joe was representing Jeff in a law suit that she really knew little about but thought it had something to do with the new stadium project. She asked me at that time if she might speak privately for a moment and before the sentence was completely out of her mouth Tiger took the cue and like a real gentleman he quickly called to AJ and asked if he might help in the kitchen.

As soon as Tiger was out of hearing range Betz whispered to me that she wanted to fully cooperate with me to aid the investigation. She told me that Jeff Watley and his wife Karen had also been guests at the party the Saturday after Thanksgiving. The following Saturday night Billy Joe had told her they were going to a pre-Christmas party at the Watley's house but when they got their it was just them and the Watleys relaxing in the hot tub which, after several glasses of Champagne had led to a swap party where she had had sex with Jeff and Karen had done Billy Joe and then the two men watched while Betz and Karen got real friendly in the hot tub. She said that swapping was something that she and Billy Joe did "occasionally" to "blow off a little steam". She also added that she had not seen or heard from either Karen or Jeff since the swing party other than they called on New Years day to offer good luck in the coming year.

I thought it was real interesting that I could put three of the four suspects with Billy Joe at the Saturday party just a few weeks before the death threat.

Unfortunately, my goal had been to separate out the suspects not blend them all into a conspiracy.

AJ had to call Dutch to the table twice to get him out of his "cave" as she referred to his office. Dinner was absolutely delicious and as soon as it was done the three of us women headed to the kitchen. Our goal was to get the dishes done and the kitchen cleaned up before we ran out of energy from the hugely satisfying meal. Tiger, the good little guard he was parked himself with a cup of coffee at the dining room table where with one eye he could watch Betz in the kitchen and the other eye could monitor the front door which would be the closest thing there was to an immediate threat on her life. Dutch, of course, wandered back to his cave.

When we slaves were done with the kitchen chores we joined Tiger at the table and AJ took out this extremely frustrating card game for us to play called "Uno". An hour later and hopelessly stuck in fourth place I was quite delighted when Dutch emerged long enough to call me into his office.

He was quite proud of his work. It all ran on his huge computer monitor and it was now much better video quality then the original fuzzy security tapes. It was still in black and white. He had made one composite file that showed Betz entering the house, then switched to Betz inside the house, then finally showed Betz getting dressed and hopping into her car as she was leaving. We now could view the entire sequence without changing tapes. That though was just the first part of Dutch's technical triumph. Down at the bottom of the computer screen there was a control box and using his mouse Dutch was able to start, stop, go forward, go backwards, speed it up, slow it down, freeze it, and infinitely magnify any portion of it. He showed me how to do all of these things but then took back control because there was something very important he wanted to show me. He fast forwarded the tape to a spot he wanted and then stopped the tape where it showed Betz, nude now, getting the wine bottle out of the refrigerator. It was as close to a full frontal shot as there was. He asked me to tell him what I saw. I briefly described the scene.

"No" he said, "What do you see about Betz?"

"She looks happy" I said not knowing what he was going for.

"No" Dutch said, "What is she wearing?"

"She is naked" I exclaimed.

"Really?" he said as if stunned by my answer, "Look closer."

"O.K." I said, "I think I see earrings, her left hand has two rings, her right wrist has a watch."

"A WATCH!!!" I said way too loud. I checked and the door to the cave was closed.

"Exactly!" Dutch proudly stated, "now watch further."

He forwarded the tape a scant few frames at a time to where Betz had turned her body and her watch was facing a counter and on the counter was a small sleek black electric can opener, and on the surface of the can opener there was a brief flash of lighter color. Dutch pointed the mouse thingy and drew a square around the can opener surface. When he clicked the next button the computer monitor filled with the black surface of the appliance. He fiddled with all the controls until we could clearly see a reflection of her watch in the surface. He drew another square and magnified again and blew that up. It was very grainy but again he started fidgeting with the dials. The reflection slowly came into blurry view but eventually Dutch got it so that we could clearly read a reverse image of the time showed on Betz's watch. It was a digital and it clearly said "10:25".

I was elated. I hugged Dutch which was, for me, showing a lot of emotion. I really try to hold it inside.

Dutch asked me if I owned a DVD player. I told him I did and he stuck a blank DVD into a slot on his computer and started copying the movie to the DVD for me.

I mentioned to Dutch that the next step would be to locate the watch itself. He told me that he could help with that because he had already located it. I asked him about this and he said that when he had come out for dinner he had specifically looked at Betz wrist to see if she was wearing the watch and she, in fact, had the same watch on right now. I explained to him that the next thing to do was find out how accurately she kept the watch set. I used the phone in his office to call the broadcast time which is extremely accurate and set my own watch to that time.

Once again I thanked Dutch for his efforts and slid the two original VCR tapes as well as the new DVD into my briefcase.

"Now watch me in action" I winked.

Back in the living room I said my good byes to everyone. I glanced at my own watch as I was putting my jacket on to cover it from view hoping that Betz had not noticed me looking at it.

"What time is it Betz?" I asked.

She looked at her wrist and quickly stated the time in digital preciseness. Tiger, of course, being the helpful gentleman he was, also shouted out the time but I clearly heard Betz answer and the digital exactness of her answer promised that her watch was accurate to within one minute.

I smiled as I was leaving. The evening had worked out wonderfully. I had calibrated the time stamp now so that I was now quite certain that Billy Joe had speaking to the telephone owned by the Katrina victim lawyer Travis Solter when Betz had overheard the threat. Of course I couldn't prove that it was actually Travis on the phone at the time but it had been an eleven minute conversation so that was way too long for a "not home" or "wrong number" or "I'll have him call you."

CHAPTER-07.

Saturday morning. Yes, I know you have the day off, but I own my own business so I never get a day off. Besides, right now I had two bosses and both thought they had my full attention so I had to keep both of them thinking that I was diligently getting to the bottom of their mysteries. I felt fairly confident that Billy Joe and his kids would be at home for a good part of the day, so I wanted to go over to his place and give him a false update of my progress to date and possibly have an opportunity to speak with the two kids a little.

Bubby answered the door and seemed to recognize me. He let me in but told me that Billy Joe was with a client. Bubby took me into the family room and sat me at the end of the couch. He picked up a game controller and resumed his video entertainment. I tried carrying on a conversation with him. It is not that he was being purposefully rude, he was just a teenager lost in a video game so all questions were treated to one-word answers being either "yes" or "no." I learned nothing other than his sister was not at home and he would be leaving soon. It did seem a little strange that he was not more interested in helping me if I were the person hired to find his missing mother.

Eventually we heard noise in the entryway, and Bubby screamed out "Dad, there's someone here for you!"

I stayed where I was but listened as the front door opened and then closed wishing I could get a peek at the "client" Billy Joe was saying good-bye to. Shortly Billy Joe poked his head into the room. Seeing it was me he invited me back to his office.

His first question wasn't "Have you found her?" It should have been. Instead he asked "What can I do for you?"

It's not that the question was inappropriate, it is just that he sounded like I was a potential client that he did not want to deal with at the time but was unwilling to be rude to.

"I just came by to give you an update" I told him.

He smiled, got me into the same chair I had sat in before with him, and we started what turned out to be a rather long meeting. Because I knew I was now on his security tapes, the first thing I told him was that I had been in the house the previous day. He seemed unconcerned with that but questioned whether I had found anything useful. I admitted I had found very little that might help me find his wife. I gave him a fake update that included checking her phone records and credit card activity. It was a lie, but I told him there had been no activity on either. I did not tell him that my own corporate card had taken a big hit in the last few days. I told him that I had gotten a police friend of mine to put her car on the watch list. This too was untrue, I knew exactly where her car was. He challenged me on this reminding me that he did not want the police brought in. I told him that I had told the cops that the car was one he owned but that one of his staffers drove all the time and it had been stolen.

This seemed to appease him. I switched the subject and asked him about Betz and her friends. I mean I knew about her tennis partner, and I also knew she was involved in several charities, but I pressed him for details about who these women (or men) might be and how to contact them. I pressed him a little more about their daily schedule, he thinking I wanted to know what she did when she was alone and I secretly hoping to find a block of time when I could get into the house and copy the hard drives.

He had to go through an address book and after about three pages I simply asked him if I could take the address book and make copies of it. He quickly agreed to this and as I was putting the address book in my briefcase I took out the two original security tapes and returned them to Billy Joe. I did tell him that I had copied them, but also told him that they had yielded few clues I could pursue.

He was an attorney, and I could use this as a fulcrum into his business affairs. It would have been better if he were a practicing prosecuting attorney in criminal trials because most of the times that lawyers get into trouble is when they convict someone who comes after them for retribution, but, divorce lawyers also got a bit of bitter retribution especially if the wife was suspected of bedding down with the lawyer while the husband was forced to pay his fees. Billy Joe got on his computer and printed me out a calendar which covered the past year. It was basically his court appearances with the names of the parties involved and the dates. I knew there would be a good deal more because many of the cases would never go as far as actual court time, but it was a start, and I was glad to have it.

We talked about what my next moves might be. Not surprisingly Billy Joe seemed to want to control my actions. He strongly suggested which of her friends I might talk to in the coming days. I could not put my finger on it exactly, but I thought he was giving me busy work but he did give me three names of women with whom Betz had recently collaborated on charity projects. I mean did he actually want me to find Betz, or, was I on staff simply to prove he had done his best to find her even if I came up empty? He asked me if I had checked with the local hospitals in case she was currently lying in some bed with a head injury. I explained that I had already done that and assured him that she was neither in a local hospital or any of the local morgues. Our little meeting wound down as I asked if I could talk with his children. He readily agreed, but told me his daughter was out of the house for the day and when we went to interview Bubby we found he had left the house while we were in the office.

Back at my abode the first thing I did was make a copy of the entire address book through the modern ease of a scanner attached to my computer. Once the names were all loaded onto the computer I then printed the whole thing off, stapled it, and put the copies in my case file. I then went through the address book to see if anything stuck out. It was obviously an address book that Billy Joe shared with Betz as it contained his business contacts, her charity contacts, and lots of friends. Unfortunately they weren't coded in any way I could discover so lots of the names meant nothing to me. The four men Billy Joe had been speaking with that I had done the background check on were all in the book. Betz tennis partner was in the book. The three names that Billy Joe had suggested I check out were in the book. Alarmingly, I found one other name of interest in the address book. The name was Anne D'Lorna and she was the woman whom Betz had told me she had stayed with right after leaving Billy Joe. Betz had told me that there was no way Billy Joe would know Anne or have any way to contact her but here was her name, phone number, and address right in their address book.

I got on the phone with Betz and asked her to give me the skinny on D'Lorna. I learned that Anne was on the board of directors for a Dallas based non-profit that taught reading to illiterate adults. All members of that particular board of directors were volunteers and did not work daily at the school. They met once a month to set policy and watch the budget plus they helped plan and run the fund raising events. Here is where Betz figured in. For as long as anyone could remember the biggest fund raising event for the non-profit was an annual luncheon where they would bring in a semi-celebrity to accept an award and make a speech while the wealthy socialites ate bland chicken and paid two-hundred dollars a plate. While the socialites were there the board tried to extract a little more cash from them several different ways. The most popular of these methods was a charity auction. Anne had been in charge of the charity auction for the past five years and she always gathered together three or four volunteers to search out auction items which might be dinner for two donated by a local restaurant, or autographed books by famous authors donated by the publishers, or guest passes to a local golf tournament, or a favorite – a day at the spa sponsored by the spa owner, or for that matter just about anything the helpers might convince anyone to donate. Betz had been one of Anne's volunteers for this event for the last two years. She claimed to really enjoy it and also suggested that she was pretty good at separating merchants from their merchandise.

Betz told me that she had first met Anne at one of the annual luncheons where she had attended simply as a guest but had happened to be sat at the same table with Anne. Anne had talked to her throughout the luncheon, and Anne had really enjoyed working as the auctioneer. They exchanged phone numbers and Betz was instantly recruited for the next years event.

According to Betz Anne D'Lorna was a lonely woman with plenty of money so she was exactly what the non-profits were after. Anne's father had started a small wireless telecommunications company about five years before cell phones dominated the landscape. Through mergers and buy-outs he lost the company eight or nine years ago but ended up with around three-hundred million dollars. The tax man took a good chunk of that away with his death and just when they got that settled Anne's mother also died. Once again the tax man stepped in and at thirty years old Anne found herself an orphan without siblings who had almost one-hundred million dollars that she had done absolutely nothing to earn. She had paid only two-hundred thousand for a nice but not glamorous house in a nice but ritzy neighborhood. She had then dumped most of the rest of the money into CDs and lived very, very comfortably on the interest a good deal of which went to her favorite non-profits.

Betz had run to her the day she fled Billy Joe because she knew Anne had the room to put her up for a few days and also because she had thought Billy Joe did not know her. According to Betz, Anne was now thirty-seven years old, still quite wealthy, still involved in a few favorite non-profits, quite beautiful, healthy, happy.

I got the address for the D'Lorna home from the address book and ran a quick Mapsco on my computer. It was a Dallas address not far from SMU (Southern Methodist University) in the Highland Park section. The area was filled with nice old houses, front lawns with Hispanics working all day long to tend them, and speed bumps along the streets. Within a mile of SMU most of the old mansions had been converted into frat houses and student rentals but Anne's house was a few blocks removed from that where everything was still private residence.

I wondered where Saturday had gone because it was almost 6:00 P.M. when I nudged the Taurus over the last speed bump near her house. Immediately I knew something was wrong because there was crime scene tape all over her yard and about half a dozen cars with flashing lights clogging the street. The first thing I noticed was that there was no ambulance but there was a coroners wagon. Uh oh. The young uniform would not let me cross the crime scene tape at first but I found out from the crowd of neighbors that had gathered that they had found a dead body. Many in the crowd claimed to know Anne and several were currently praying that the body was not hers.

I stood along the tape by the uniform until a detective came over to talk to him. I introduced myself and produced my PI license. He let me past the tape but only allowed me a few feet beyond that so that we could hold a private conversation. I, of course, could not tell him who I worked for, but was able to tell him enough so that he understood that I had a real interest in the case, and as I had a license he let me into the fray.

There were maybe twenty people in the house but it was eerily quiet for a crowd that size. Everyone was official. I knew enough to not touch anything.

Anne D'Lorna, or what was left of her was in the living room. It was a large comfortable room and it appeared the furniture normally had all been grouped in the middle as a conversation pit but it had all been shoved back out of the way so that there was a large empty space in the middle of the room. There was a heavy wooden beam running along the ceiling. Apparently the perpetrators had been in the house for quite a while. They had drilled two large holes through the ceiling beam and then run some heavy rope through the two holes. The drill and ladder they used for this operation had been casually tossed against the back wall of the room along with some of the displaced furniture. Anne's nude body was hung by the spread ankles from the two ropes in the beam. Her wrists were tied together behind her back. As she hung her dangling hair from her head could not quite reach the floor.

I happened to arrive on the scene shortly following the senior detective who had been assigned the case and he was near the body when I first saw it. A young studious looking woman in a white smock and rubber gloves was giving him the facts of the horrendous incident. She was reading from her note pad but really didn't need to as she had just catalogued most of the data herself. As I approached she was mentioning that there were three chairs arranged in a circle around the strung up corpse indicating that there had been three bad guys there and they had been there for a good deal of time. They had not been in a hurry. They had moved the furniture out of the way, then strung the woman up while she was very much alive, then at their leisure had gone to the dining room to take three of the chairs from there and carried them into the living room and set them up surrounding the woman. There were five separate acts of violence the scientist conveyed to the detective.

She held up a baggie which contained a regular pair of pliers they had found at the scene. She also indicated the bare vagina of the hanging D'Lorna and suggested they had used the pliers to yank out her pubic hair. This suggestion was backed up by a scattering of short curly hairs she had gathered up from the floor surrounding the area.

Secondly she indicated that based on the stains on the carpet and the smell of her hair it was pretty obvious that the three men had then urinated on her face and let it drip down into her hair. The scientist made sure to tell the detective that she had gathered several samples and could not be sure until she got back to the lab but by smell she was sure it was urine.

The third thing she had pointed out was that a metal poker from the fire place set had been used to thoroughly beat her. The scientist held the tool up to several different bruises on Anne's body matching the bruise to the shape and size of the tool. The bruises covered all of her body. They had been quite thorough in their application of pain.

Next the scientist showed the detective a large plastic bag containing a long extension cord that had been used to power a regular old-style soldering iron which was also in the bag. She told the cop that she had found it still plugged in and still turned on tossed to the floor near the body. She showed him not only which wall socket it had been plugged into but also showed him the large burn spot in the carpet where she had found it. She suggested that if the body had been discovered perhaps fifteen or twenty minutes later the place probably would have burned and perhaps that was the intent of the perpetrators but apparently no accelerant had been used. She then demonstrated using a pen rather than the soldering iron itself how the three men had used the soldering iron to burn the helpless woman. They had started on her legs between the ankle and knee. She suggested that they started there simply because it was as high on her body as they could comfortably reach bound as she was. Each burn was about half an inch oval in shape that cleanly matched the tip of the soldering iron. The burns were spaced out at approximately one burn for every two inches of flesh. They had started by circling each leg between the ankle and knee and worked their way down her inverted body along her thighs to her torso and about half way down her trunk. At that point the burns stopped and the scientist had no explanation for why they had stopped. The detective told the scientist that they had obviously been interrogating D'Lorna and it was probably at the stopping point where they had learned whatever it was they were after.

At that point they had gone onto the final torture. They had pulled a clear plastic bag over her head and used duct tape to secure it around her neck. The three had then waited as she breathed up all the oxygen in the bag and finally died. Once she had expired they had ripped the bag off of her and left most of the duct tape on her throat. It was the scientists suggestion that at that point the three perpetrators had left the scene.

Anne D'Lorna had died a terrible death.

CHAPTER-08.

Senior Detective Eric Samuels thanked the scientist for her good preliminary work and succinct report. He pointed out to her which things he wanted photographed, then he turned to face me. He was short, probably ten inches less then my own height, but he was very powerfully built. I guessed his age at about fifty. He looked serious and studious with his black framed glasses on but as he turned to me he slid the glasses off his face and into his breast pocket in a smooth well-practiced and natural looking move.

He asked me who I was and what I was doing there. As I gave him a brief story that did not implicate my clients but let him know that I had come to the house to interview D'Lorna for a current investigation, he looked me up and down and I could just tell he was cataloguing me, imprinting my appearance in his memory. I just somehow knew he would never forget me and would be able to recognize me on sight for ever. Calmly he asked for my card which I produced for him from my briefcase. He told me to stay and look as long as I wanted to but to be in his office in twelve hours prepared to "chat" about my case and to bring with me any pertinent evidence I might be in possession of. He handed me one of his own cards and without waiting for any response from me he turned to the next person and was immediately buried in a conversation with that person.

I looked at my watch. It was 7:15 P.M. I was required to be at the police station about dawn on the next morning which was a Sunday. So much for sleeping in on my day off.

What had started out as a fairly easy case had just turned very ugly and dangerous. Nobody stopped me when I took out my camera and started taking digital records of the carnage. I shot most of the room where Anne's lifeless body hung. I crossed into the dining room and shot a picture of the dining set missing the three straight-backed chairs. Along the wall in the dining room was a large buffet cabinet and along the top of it I saw something I recognized from long ago. With my digital I took several shots. What I was interested in was a set of beer mugs that had become fairly popular in America as a trade item shortly after World War One. My parents had owned a set that they kept proudly lined up on the mantle over the fire place. As I recalled my parents set there were five ceramic mugs made in Germany and decorated with young Slavic men and women. The scenes on them were not only painted on but actually done in relief into the clay that had been formed into the mugs. The five mugs were graduated in size with the smallest capable of holding about three ounces of liquid and the largest being a full liter stein. Each of the mugs also had a little cone shaped aluminum topper. It required that you use your thumb to press a little flange that opened the topper so that the mug was uncovered while you took a sip. The set of mugs brought back a bad memory. When about ten years old I had been alone and bored in the living room of our house with my basketball and I swear I didn't do it but suddenly the smallest mug laid in shattered plaster on the floor. My parents had punished me for that but forever then left the four mugs on the mantle not even repositioning them so that in the future everyone who saw the mugs would clearly see that there was one missing. If my dear mother had simply spread the four remaining mugs out a little nobody would have ever been the wiser.

What caught my eye about this particular set of mugs was that they were positioned along the top of the buffet in the same manner. One of the mugs was missing. In my case I had broken the smallest one. In this case it was the largest that was missing but again the remaining four mugs had not been redistributed to cover the fact that one was missing. I examined the top of the buffet and could clearly see the dust ring where the largest mug would have been sitting. I photographed the top of the buffet hoping to clearly indicate the missing space for the fifth mug. I looked around the front rooms and did not find the missing mug. I also did not find a familiar pile of broken shards indicating the mug had been smashed. Of course all could be quite innocent. The fifth mug could have been removed two or three days ago for cleaning or repair.

I was close to panic but suppressed it because I had something very important to do before fleeing the scene. At my size and with my big old blonde hair I am fairly easy to recognize, and I knew what would come next as I fled the house. I looked through the drawers of the buffet cabinet in the dining room until I found some dark green large cloth napkins. I took one out and wrapped it around my head like a scarf. I then took my large dark glasses out of my briefcase and donned them. I wandered through the kitchen until I found a back door and quietly slipped out into the semi-darkness. I followed the driveway around the house and out front where I tried to mill into the crowd before I was spotted by any of the reporters and film crews that were now clogging the scene in front of the house. Fortune smiled upon me and I made it to my Taurus without any direct attention. I knew there would be a good deal of danger for anyone connected with the case and I certainly did not want people catching a glimpse of me on the news that night.

Luckily I had parked several houses down the street because the media trucks and emergency vehicles now closed all lanes of the small street near the house. As it were I had to drive over some neighbors well edged lawn for thirty or forty feet to get out of the melee. I pointed the Taurus north and my trusted steed got me the hell out of there.

You know how most people can't eat after seeing something as disturbing as I had just witnessed? Well, I am not one of those people. I stopped at a MacDonald's and went inside. I only ordered items from the dollar menu. By the time I left I had gone back to the counter twice and had spent nearly twelve bucks.

Fortunately, when I got back to the house Laura was gone. I fully expected she was already at work. I locked the door, I checked every window. I turned on every light I could find. I purposefully did not turn on anything like a television or radio because I wanted to be able to hear any creepy noise that might be produced by bad guys about to break in. I placed my briefcase on my desk and opened it. The first thing I did was take out my gun and make sure it was fully loaded. I took out my pepper spray and sat it down on my desk right next to the gun. I picked up the spray again and gave it a good shake and put it back down.

Then, the house prepared, I put on a pot of coffee. I stayed in the kitchen until it was done with all the gurgling and sputtering. Finally, completely prepared now, I sat down at my desk to go to work.

Detective Samuels had told the tech that the perps had been interrogating Anne. I was positive he was correct about that. Samuels though probably had no idea what information they were trying to get from the woman. I was pretty sure the word "Betz" had probably come up in their violent conversation. This had to be more though than what was on the surface. There was simply too much pain, too much violence, too much gore for a simple missing wife case. My first instinct was flight. I mean I seriously considered gathering up Betz and Dutch and AJ and Laura and moving to Indiana or the Grand Caymans immediately, but, there was really no reason to do so. It was really quite simple. Betz had told me that Anne D'Lorna did not know where she was or that I was working for her. If Betz were telling me the truth it was a sad but simple fact that no matter what persuasive techniques they had used when questioning Anne she could not give them information she did not have. On the other hand, if Betz were in on the deal and was playing me then the bad guys would have known about me for several days now so there would be no reason to go through D'Lorna to get to me. At this time, no matter how scared I was, the most constructive thing I could do was continue working on the case. The only other possibility was that the D'Lorna incident had nothing to do with Betz and Billy Joe and the timing of the event was just a coincidence. I didn't believe that for even a second.

CHAPTER-09.

I arrived at the Dallas Police sub-station just about the time the sun rose over this fresh new day. I hadn't slept a wink. I had tried but I could not get the image of Anne's nude tortured lifeless body out of my mind. Laura had arrived home just an hour before I was due to wake up so I simply kissed her on the cheek and sent her to bed. I did not divulge to her the reason for my insomnia.

In the last 24 hours this case had gone way beyond what I was prepared to handle. With a torture/murder of one of the characters in the drama it had become a police matter. No matter what confidentiality my two clients might reasonably expect it was time for me to jump over that blue wall and land squarely on the side that cooperates fully with police investigations. That is why I arrived at the police station not only on time but also loaded down with evidence to share.

There are two types of police stations in America. There are the brand new sleek modern buildings built recently from tax payer dollars that are well run and well built but a lot like modern businesses preferring rows of cubicles and carpeted hallways. This, however, was not that type of police station. The other type of station is an old one, the type you see so many times on television. Where I entered the department was dominated by large high reception desk manned by a mean old sergeant who wanted desperately to still be a part of the police department but hated working reception which was the only duty his war wounds would now permit.

Beyond the reception desk, if you were able to make it so far, was a large open area with detective's desks scattered around mostly in pairs and mostly cluttered and un-kept. Surrounding this open area was a ring of offices that were actually little rooms with doors that could be closed. I am sure that down one hall would be interrogation rooms and just beyond them a couple of stout holding cells. Somewhere on the floor would be a small room crowded with a copy machine, a coffee pot brewing the strongest coffee in town and an old box of stale donuts. A civilian volunteer led me to the office of Senior Detective Eric Samuels.

I had to awkwardly stand for two minutes sort of half in and half out of his door while he finished business with someone else. He apologized to me for that as he got me into the only guest chair in his cramped space. He offered me coffee which I readily accepted. To accommodate me he picked up the phone and told someone to fetch it but did not wait for it to arrive before beginning our chat.

We went through a few getting acquainted pleasantries while awaiting the coffee but when it was delivered he told the young volunteer who had brought it to shut the door on her way out. In the closed cramped office Eric Samuels got right down to business.

An hour later I was back in my car having divulged all I knew about both of my clients. Samuels was pretty impressed that I was contracted to working for both of the parties. He understood exactly how it had happened and did not blame me for it at all. He seemed quite interested in all the material I had gathered especially the luds from the phone calls. It was not like he couldn't get the luds himself, it was more that he was impressed that I had been able to get them and had even thought to go after them. He handed all four video tapes to a tech and had quick copies made. He did not look at them while I was there but he listened as I patiently explained what each contained. He looked at the printout of the pictures I had taken of the beer mugs and patiently listened to my story of there needing to be a fifth that was recently missing. I had made a copy on diskette of the digital images of all the shots I had taken and he gladly accepted those. He was always the professional but he was less impressed with the evidence I could give him than I expected him to be.

You see he was not at all interested in my case, but he was quite curious as to how my case had led me to be at Anne D'Lorna's house less than an hour after she had died and almost as soon as he had arrived himself. He sensed that our cases were related and wanted to use that to his advantage. Samuels told me he wanted to interview Betz or at least have one of his people do that. He did allow my request to wait until noon so that I would have a chance to tell her about D'Lorna. I did not want Betz surprised with that piece of news while being interrogated by a cop. I gave him the details of the location of the rental. The rental actually caused a bit of a problem though because Samuel's jurisdiction ended with the county line and while he was very much in control of how things worked in Dallas county the rental was across the line into Tarrant county. So what we ended up with was that I would tell Betz about Anne, and Samuels would call me later in the day when he had arranged for someone from Fort Worth's police department to interview her.

Samuels and I talked a bit about the location of the new stadium but that too was out of his jurisdiction and neither of us knew how it tied into the mysteries we were each pursuing. The most interesting piece of news for me came when I went over the names of the four people that Billy Joe had spoken with on the phone that morning. He seemed completely uninterested in three of the names but when I mentioned the name Travis Solter, the lawyer from New Orleans, Samuels interest picked up considerably. He actually divulged to me it was a name he was familiar with and that the Dallas PD was looking at Solter as a possible in a case they were currently working on but he wouldn't give me any details about what that case involved. He did say though that he did not think it was connected to the death of D'Lorna but I had my own doubts. I mean right now I had no clue at all what was going on except that I was pretty sure it was not simply about a wife who wanted to divorce her husband. Any other active police investigations about players in my case might be and probably were connected.

Samuels and I covered another subject. He wanted to talk to Billy Joe to see if he could find any link between Billy Joe and Anne D'Lorna other than through Betz. The problem was that he did not want to blow my cover with Billy Joe so he had no reason to suspect Billy Joe, and therefore he (Samuels) could not just go and pick up Billy Joe and start questioning him. What Samuels came up with was that he told me to talk Billy Joe into going to the police to report Betz missing and he gave me one of his cards to give Billy Joe. He told me to tell Billy Joe that we were old friends and that I knew he would handle the investigation of the missing wife with discretion and keep it out of the media. He even encouraged me to accompany Billy Joe into the station house so that I could make sure he talked to Samuels and not some other cop.

Finally Samuels and I discussed the thing that had been really bugging me. We talked about the murder scene we had just investigated. To me the really frightening thing was that the three men who had committed the murder had left a ton of DNA all over the place and done almost nothing to cover it up. That meant that they were either really stupid or didn't care at all about getting caught. Detective Samuels though had a theory to cover that. In his opinion, and I have to say he is probably correct, the three men were not afraid of leaving DNA because they felt pretty secure that they would never be caught, or if caught, could not be punished. That meant that they were from some other country and most likely one which did not have an extradition treaty with the United States. That also meant that they were probably already back in their country or well on their way there by now. Unfortunately it also indicated that this was way more involved than a missing wife case because bringing in three killers from out of the country to interrogate and kill one person would have been very expensive. There was a huge amount of money being made that was somehow connected to my case. We had just not yet figured out where the money came from or what it was for. We also, of course, did not know who was making the money or, more importantly, who might be in jeopardy of losing it if Betz left Billy Joe.

There was one more scenario that Eric Samuels had already come up with that he shared with me. It was possible that the murder had been committed by local talent and they had been casual about leaving evidence because they had intended to destroy it. The soldering iron had been left on and the carpet was, in fact, burnt where they had left it. Had the scene been left undisturbed for perhaps less than one more hour the entire house might have burned down. Instead of torching the house immediately the delay would have given the killers a chance to be somewhere else establishing alibi when the fire started. It had been a lucky stroke that Anne D'Lorna had received that day in the mail a registered letter that required that the postman get her signature. The postman had found the front door unlocked and gotten curious. Had it not been for that letter, I would probably have been the next one to visit her house and by then it might have been nothing but a pile of ashes. So Samuels clearly now believed that the first theory was more likely, but he had not eliminated the possibility that this had been done by local boys.

I parked the Taurus in front of my own house around nine A.M. It was too early to go see Betz at the rental, and it was too late for me to catch a much needed nap. I hopped into the shower and stayed in almost half an hour.

It was a Sunday morning. I would have preferred to call Mandy on her cell phone because she would probably be at church and I did not want to leave a message on her answering machine, but I looked in my rolodex and could not find a cell number for her. I took a chance and called her home phone. Lucky for me she picked up after the second ring. I invited her for dinner on Monday night before I even asked the favor she knew was coming. I begged her to pull luds on Travis Solter for the past six months and also asked her to get the past month or two on the other three suspects Billy Joe had called. She kept me on the phone about twenty minutes making absolutely sure I knew how hard it would be for her to gather her data and what a huge risk she would be taking. Eventually though she did agree to do it but then she told me that she was really tired of lasagna but would love it if we could have stuffed Cornish hen. I was in no position to argue but that really put me in a bind. I mean I am a really good cook as long as I could buy it frozen and simply shove it in the oven. I did know someone special though who was practically famous for her stuffed Cornish hen, and started to wonder if Mandy could have been aware of that as well.

Laura had worked Saturday night until the jiggle joint closed at four this morning so, not surprisingly, I found her sound asleep in our bed. As quietly as I could I slid into the bed behind her and snuggled into the spoon position behind her. For several minutes I just held her there fighting the tremendous urge to simply spend the day without moving again. By nibbling on her right ear and whispering louder and louder I got her awake and shortly urged her into a standing position next to our bed, and pointed her at the bath room. While she went potty I sprinted into the kitchen to get her a cup of coffee and have it perfect and ready at her seat at the dining room table before she came out.

She knew I needed a favor or I would not have dared to wake her. It appeared by the look on her face though that she had no intention of making it easy on me. I hemmed and hawed a bit and she requested that I get to the point. Surprisingly she seemed quite all right with my request that she not only cook Cornish hens for us and Mandy the next night but she also made no argument when I requested that she do the shopping. She did accept the wad of cash I shoved at her to pay for the groceries. That unpleasant business done we spent about thirty minutes talking with her telling stories of unfulfilled men at her chosen place of employment and me bringing her up to date on my case. I would not, of course, tell her about the horrendous death scene I had just witnessed, so there was really precious little I could tell her.

I drove over to the rental and found Bear and Dutch in the living room watching a B-rated movie that featured scantily clad well developed young women driving fast cars in a reckless manner. Boys and their toys! Betz and AJ were in the kitchen sitting at the table drinking coffee. I called the men into the kitchen with them because I didn't want to tell the story of Anne's death more than once. I got right to the point choosing not to suppress any of the gory details. It was bad for Betz and she took it hard. I probably could have told the tale a little softer but I wanted her to hear every detail because if she was involved I wanted to see her reaction. She was genuinely startled which I expected and she seemed totally scared for her own life which, to me at least, seemed to mean that she was not involved. Still it was a difficult call on my part. She showed genuine panic and the flight urge grasped her tightly. She wanted to load up her purse with cash and get in the car and drive as fast as she could in any direction. AJ calmed her down a good deal and I actually saw Bear sneak the car keys out of Betz's purse.

I talked to Bear and requested that he call his agency and get more guards. I wanted two trained guards with Betz at all times from here on out, or at least until I could figure out what was going on. Betz was the client I was actually working for here and my primary duty was to protect her. I could not stay with her myself and also get to the bottom of the mystery, but I could arrange for more protection. Bear made a phone call and reported that he could get more help in a couple of hours. That done I talked to Dutch and he agreed to stay at the rental at least until the second guard arrived. He also slid his jacket open so I could see that he was packing.

I probably shouldn't have done this but I was really pissed off because of D'Lorna and was pretty sure that Betz was not tied to her death but felt it a good possibility that Billy Joe was up to his arm-pits in the mess. Therefore I took the opportunity to review with Betz what I had found on the internet about her bank accounts. I had found several bank accounts that had Betz or Billy Joe's names on them. Specifically there were two accounts that had just the name Billy Joe Jenton on them so Betz couldn't do much about them. There were three joint accounts that were each titled "Billy Joe Jenton or Betz Jenton." These three accounts each had several hundred-thousand dollars in balance. Finally there was one more account that had only the name Betz Jenton on it, and all of these accounts were at the same bank. I explained to Betz that she had access to the joint accounts just like Billy Joe did, but that she could not touch any of the money in the accounts with his name only on them. Likewise, I explained, he could not touch the account that had just her name. I then gave her the number of the customer service department for the bank and told her that one of the services they offered was that you could transfer money from one account to another over the phone as long as you had signer rites on the accounts. I suggested she borrow the cell phone that was registered to the guard service just in case. I then sat there and listened as she called the customer service number. By the time she hung up the three joint accounts each had a positive balance of one dollar and her separate account had one point three million. Politely she thanked me for my foresight in the matter. I left there feeling very smug and quite pleased with myself.

When I fired up the Taurus the radio kicked on and since I had it permanently dialed into a '60s rock and roll station it was currently playing The Who's "Don't Get Fooled Again." I love that song, but I turned the radio off because I had to practice all the lies I was about to tell Billy Joe, my other client. I pulled up to the Jenton house at exactly the correct time. Billy Joe was walking some man I had never met to his car and saying good bye just as I pulled up. We went through the fake social scene where Billy Joe took full control and introduced me by my name but told the man I was Billy Joe's cousin and that I had come over to take the kids to church. He lied to me when he told me the man was there because they were opponents on a divorce case and they were trying to work out an out-of-court settlement. I nearly froze as Billy Joe introduced the guy as "Travis Solter." We shook hands but Solter wouldn't look me in the eye.

I happened to notice that Solter was driving a new Mercedes with a Louisiana vanity plate that said "SOLTY1". His sleek new ride made my old Taurus look pretty grim. As Solter drove down the driveway I followed Billy Joe into the house and into his office. Without even asking Billy Joe refreshed his own drink and made me one. I could see Solter's half-empty glass on the edge of the desk. Bourbon and water at noon on a Sunday. Forgive me God. It tasted delicious and I really needed it.

I wanted to come right to the point but for the purpose of keeping everything straight I had to start with a lie. I told Billy Joe that I had made several calls to women I had found in their address book. I tossed out a couple of names just to see his reaction, and told him that I had spoken with each on the phone to see if she had seen Betz after the day she went missing. Then I told him that I had made a list of three possible women Betz might have run to but that I was unable to reach on the phone, so I had decided to go to their homes and interview them in person. Just to make my lie a little better I put Anne third on my list and went through the motions of telling Billy Joe about the other two I had fictitiously placed on the list and the brief "interview" I had conducted with each. Billy Joe seemed quite uninterested. Then I told him the name of the third woman.

When the name "Anne D'Lorna" came out of my mouth I caught two quick reactions from Billy Joe. First, there was a very brief flash in his eyes and I swear they changed color for a second but he quickly got it under control. Secondly, but at the exact same time his right hand twitched so hard that I heard the ice in his glass rattle. Still, though Billy Joe told me he did not know Anne D'Lorna but suspected Betz had met her through one of her many charities or at the tennis club.

I reported to Billy Joe that I had interviewed the first two women and then headed over to the D'Lorna house. At this point my story could stop being lie and start being truth. I told him exactly the truth about what I had found at the murder scene. I even detailed the tortures the woman had endured except I left out that they had yanked out all her pubic hair with a pliers. The reason I left that part out, of course, was that if Billy Joe ever relayed the story to someone else, and included that detail, it would mean that he had heard it from someone else.

There was what appeared to be a good deal of concern on Billy Joe's face as I told him the gory details so I used that to segue into asking him to go to the police. At this point he pretty much had to agree to go to them and report her as missing. He told me he was hopeful that Betz had no connection to D'Lorna but also agreed that she was in way too much danger to not report her as missing. Besides, if she were actually missing and he did not report her as such it would tend to make him look involved.

I slipped him Eric Samuels card and offered to escort him to the station. He asked me when we should go to talk with Samuels and I suggested that we go immediately. He could not come up with a good reason not to go but he told me he had to make a couple of quick calls before he could leave and asked if I might wait in the living room. Gambling here I took the chance to ask him if I might go up to their bed room to collect one more thing I might just need. For dramatic effect I took a small sip of my bourbon before continuing on. I told Billy Joe that the police would probably want a DNA sample for Betz "just in case". I mentioned that Betz had played tennis that morning and since she was going to be seen in her tennis outfit it was sure that she had shaved her legs that morning. The freshest DNA sample I could think of would be on her razor. I asked Billy Joe if I could slip up to their bathroom and grab the razor. He was as good at this game as I, or perhaps even better. For dramatic effect he not only took a sip of his drink but once again I saw that single tear roll down his cheek. I wondered (not out loud) if all lawyers could do that on command. Billy Joe told me to go ahead and look for the razor as he picked up the telephone and started dialing.

I was carrying with me a prop I almost never use, a big old floppy purse. I hate carrying a purse but being born a female I had the right to carry one whenever I wanted. This was a time where I could use it to my advantage. It was my intention to scarf up her razor as planned, but another part of my plan was to sneak into Billy Joe's closet and shove a couple of more tapes into my purse. It would be interesting to catalogue the entire collection, but for now I just wanted a couple more to see if my first two random samples had been lucky or if there were more tapes with Betz on them. I figured I could get three of four tapes easily into my empty bag. The real problem would be that there would be three or four less tapes in the pile on the floor of Billy Joe's closet and I didn't want him to notice.

At the top of the stairs I went directly to their bed room and then into their bath room where I found and collected a pink disposable razor from the soap dish of the bath tub. I turned, went back to the bed room. Made sure the bed room door was open, peeked out into the hall, listened quietly, could actually hear Billy Joe talking on the phone but could not hear what he was saying. I turned and crossed the room back to Billy Joe's closet. I slid the door open. The closet was empty. I mean not empty, there was nothing there, I mean empty full of clothes and shoes and other things that belong in the closet but absolutely no camera or tapes.

CHAPTER-10.

Fortunately Billy Joe insisted on driving his own car so that he could talk to the police and I could get on with finding Betz after introducing him to my detective friend. As I was driving I got on my cell and called Samuels to give him the heads-up that we were on our way. For the next part of the drama he would not be playing the part of a homicide investigator trying to solve the D'Lorna murder, he would be playing the part of my friend who might be able to discretely help with a missing person case, so he had to get all the D'Lorna stuff off of his desk, and he also had to instruct the desk Sergeant in what to do with us when we arrived. I have to admit it was a little creepy driving with Billy Joe trailing me. I felt like I was bent over in a short skirt with a red and white bull's eye painted on my big ass. Finally we pulled into the sub-station parking lot and found two parking slots next to each other. If this had not been a Sunday we would have had to park across the street and paid for the privilege.

The desk Sergeant made us wait seven minutes and then he led us back to Samuels office. Unfortunately for me, Samuels kicked me out as soon as he got Billy Joe into his guest chair. Before he sent me on my way though he handed me a large envelope stuffed with something, and told me to read it when I got home.

Back at the homestead I found Laura awake and listening to music. She does this rather often and when she does she really cranks it up loud. For practice she generally dances while the music is playing and often dances naked. This time however she was in a t-shirt and cut-off jeans so I could concentrate on my business rather than my lady. I was tempted to tell her about D'Lorna's death just to let her know what type of danger was out there, but she seemed so happy at the moment that I decided to let her live in blissful ignorance another day or two.

I grabbed a Diet Coke from the refrigerator and sat down at my desk with my package from Samuels. There were several different photos in the package. Eight by ten black and white glossies. Betz and Billy Joe were both represented but also were most of the rest of the folks involved with my case. I briefly looked over the pictures and set them aside because also in the package Samuels had given me was a thick ream of paper that was bank statements going back a full year on several accounts that all had Betz or Billy Joe's name on them. Just to check, I pulled out the not yet deposited check Billy Joe had given me and it was, in fact, drawn on the bank listed in Samuels reports.

As Laura's music droned on I started going over the bank statements. An hour later I had made a list of several interesting items. Unfortunately, these were simply bank statements, and I already had most of the information, but I continued to look through it in case there was something here that I had missed when I had gathered the banking information. If a check were written one could see where the money was going, but in this day and age there were more electronic transfers than checks and most of these transfers simply listed the routing number and account of where the money went to or came from so they told me how much and when but not who or why. I was able to identify the common stuff. For instance I found an account that each month was used to pay the mortgage on their house and the regular bills like electricity and cable. I found a completely different account that covered the same types of bills but did them for Billy Joe's office. Both of these accounts had been on the list of accounts I had uncovered and Betz had just drained, but now I knew what the accounts had been used for as well as the balances. Having these two separate accounts to keep the business records separated from the household expenses was not uncommon. My own life was still simple enough that I could manage it on one checking account and one savings account, but many folks kept separate accounts like this. The trouble was that I found a third account that seemed to be making very similar type payments. I could see monthly debits that would account for rent or mortgage as well as the common bills, but I could find nothing about the location of the place. Still it could be innocent. Perhaps out of generosity Billy Joe was paying the living expenses of Betz's parents. Ha ha ha.

What I also found and added to my notes was several rather hefty electronic payments that were not on a cyclical basis so would not be for regular bills rather they would be for one time expenses. Interestingly Betz had an account and lots of the special type payments seemed to come from her account. At first I thought these were probably charity donations but I didn't think that likely because with a check you have something to show to the IRS so you can deduct the charitable donations but you would never get the tax deduction from an electronic transfer.

At least with Betz I could confront her and simply ask who the payments were to and what they covered.

I did notice something else about the accounts. Several of their accounts were joint accounts meaning that either Betz or Billy Joe could transact business on the account, but they each also had one account that had just their own name on it. The one with Betz name on it had lots of undocumented and interesting activity but the account that belonged to Billy Joe showed very little of interest. There were occasional small deposits and then a specific withdrawal made just days before Christmas or Betz' birthday, or one of the children's birthday. Apparently Billy Joe took gift buying for his family seriously. I could use this information as a basis but I had to remember that Detective Samuels was able to give me everything he found but he may not have found everything. It was certainly possible that Billy Joe or Betz or both had other bank accounts that had not popped up on the police search. It would not be difficult to do using business accounts and shell corporations.

The data Samuels gave me was much more detailed than what I had gotten when I had called the banks myself. I had been able to direct Betz in emptying their joint accounts but with the details Samuels gave me I was able to plot some of their monthly expenditures which gave me a much clearer picture of how my two clients lived their lives.

I guess I had been at it for a couple of hours. I noticed the music was off and wondered how long ago Laura had stopped her dancing. Laura came into the office carrying a tray which she put down on my desk right on top of what I was working on. This was her clue that she wanted me to stop working for a while and at least communicate with her for a few minutes.

The tray was loaded down with dinner. O.K. loaded down is not appropriate, but the tray did hold two nice bowls of soup. I dug into mine wondering how I had possibly done so much work while starving as I was. We talked mostly about Mandy's next visit which was conveniently scheduled for the next evening, Monday. As we were talking Laura scooped up the photos and started looking through them. I was happy that the D'Lorna death pics were not on my desk. As she looked slowly through the stack of photos she came to one and looked at it for a long time and then told me that she recognized the man. Of course I questioned her on where she knew the man from. She told me a story of a lonely man who had wandered into her club one evening and immediately been drawn to a particular stripper. He had dropped a ton of cash on the girl that night, and showed up maybe five times in the next ten days looking for her. If she were there he would stay and spend again a lot of money on the young lady. If she were not there he would stay only long enough to have a single drink. After about two weeks the girl had moved on to another club. The man had stopped in almost every day of the following week looking for the girl but then he had stopped showing up. She handed me the photo and it was, of course, a face I recognized, Travis Solter.

CHAPTER-11.

Monday started like a typical Monday. You know what I mean. I got out of bed, tossed my robe on, headed into the kitchen where I found we were out of coffee. I headed into the shower and was good and wet when I found we had no shampoo. It was a good thing we had toilet paper or I really would have been pissed off or would that have been pissed on? Sorry. It had rained the previous night and there was a small puddle on my huge front porch. The puddle was perhaps eight feet from the front door but it was, of course, exactly where I found the morning paper. I decided to work from home as much as I could because I could not face a flat tire this early and fully expected one if I went anywhere near the Taurus.

I cracked open a can of Diet Coke to get my caffeine and sat down in my robe at my desk. I could not get my head right for working so I looked around and noticed that the cleaning fairy had not magically spruced up the office in a while so I changed my plans for the day.

I snuck into the bed room where Laura was sawing logs and quietly dropped my robe. Not wanting to make any noise I grabbed some clothing from the floor and slithered out of the room. What I had been able to grab in the dark was the same t-shirt and cut offs that Laura had been wearing the night before. I am a good deal larger than Laura so it took a lot of struggle to get the jeans up over my hips and the t-shirt hit me right at the navel leaving most of my stomach visible. Dirty hair, no coffee, tight clothing, belly hanging out, rubber gloves, a mop in one hand and a bucketful of cleaning supplies in the other. Sexy, I know. When it is too cold and rainy outside for fresh air therapy this elbow-grease therapy is a good substitute. Usually.

An hour later I was on my knees facing this one corner of the office, trying to scrub the dust off the floor using one of those sponge things that have the hard scrubbing surface on one side. It was, of course, at that very moment, with my massive ass, which was barely covered by the denim cut offs and with the loose fringe annoyingly tickling my thighs, pointing right at the door that Betz and two of her guards walked right into the office. As I said earlier, almost everyone ignores the sign on the door that invites them to walk right in. How fortunate for me that someone finally obeyed the suggestion.

I swallowed what little pride I had left and made an apology for everything from my appearance to the weather and that included not being able to offer them coffee. Bear introduced me to Zebra who was one of the two new guards. Zebra was a little smaller than Bear and Asian in appearance but still quite dapper in his tight fitting suit. We all sat in the living room and I gave Betz an update on what I had been up to the past day. She was especially interested in any news I could give her about Anne D'Lorna's slaying but I had little to give. In spite of the obvious danger involved with everything that was going on Betz was getting very anxious and quite annoyed at having to stay under cover. She desperately wanted to get back to a couple of her charities. I had to tell her "no" about half a dozen times. Fortunately Bear and Zebra backed me up completely on this.

I did take the opportunity to get out the bank statement that had her name on it and asked her about several of the large expenditures. I got the feeling I caught her off guard with the questions and it seemed she was being less than 100% truthful when she answered. It is not like she refused to answer or anything but she seemed to take a long time to think over what she was going to say and then it would be a vague answer. For instance, on one expense I asked her about she thought for a while and then told me that she had used the money to buy airline tickets for a family vacation. Then when I asked her where the vacation was she had to think for a good deal of time before giving me the answer. I didn't want to press too hard but couldn't resist asking why she had used an electronic transfer instead of writing them a check but on this one she was quick to answer that she had bought the tickets on-line from one of those auctions where you had to pay immediately if you won. Not knowing much about internet auctions I had to let that one go. Eventually though we did make it all the way through the bank statement with some type of plausible answer for each expenditure. I hardly believed most of it though.

I really had no reason to think she would lie, but my bull-shit meter works pretty well. In my line of business it is a must-have. I did not ask her any questions about the expenses on the other accounts other than to have her look them over and see if she knew of any missing accounts. She could not give me any information about any accounts I had missed. I had one little trap built in and that was that I had also included the statement from the one bank account that had the household-looking expenses but for the household I could not identify. I half expected her to be confused by the account but she said nothing at all about it. That told me she knew what the account was for but I suddenly did not trust her enough to ask her what it's purpose was.

With that business done Bear went over the days agenda while Zebra kept a good watch on my much-too-tight t-shirt. God, I wish I had put on a bra. The agenda had originally included some stops at homes of women involved in some upcoming charity events so it now had a few holes in it. I did allow that they could go out to a nice lunch as long as Betz agreed to keep her sun glasses and scarf on and also if they would do it in one of the north east suburbs. I wanted to keep them away from Dallas, Irving, and now Arlington especially around the new stadium project.

Finally they all left and I was really depressed at how the day had begun.

Sometimes though you just get lucky. I tossed on some decent clothing and hopped into the car simply planning on going to the grocery store to get some much needed supplies. Shampoo and coffee toping the list. I live on the east bound side of 183, and the best grocery store was three exits west so I had to do that thing where you go down to the nearest exit and loop under the expressway going the other direction. Just as I was getting up to speed on the west bound entry ramp I was passed by, believe it or not, a Mercedes with SOLTY1 on the back tag.

Well this was just too good to be true. I pushed the Taurus a little too fast so that I could catch up and got behind him just long enough to verify that it was Travis Solter driving the car. I eased up on the gas allowing myself to fall back a couple of car lengths and soon some other car had jumped in between us which was just what I wanted. Travis stayed on 183 just long enough to hit Highway 360 where he turned south and headed to Arlington. We were only on 360 for a couple of exits and Travis turned off at Brown Trail. He headed southwest which brought us right into the area where the real estate people were saying Billy Joe had the options. I followed as close as I dared while Solter made his familiar way through a neighborhood. I was about half a block behind praying that he had not noticed me when he pulled into a driveway. I pulled to the curb and quickly got my binoculars out of the glove box. I caught him walking into the door of a very large house. Since this had started out as a shopping trip I did not have all of tools of the trade with me but I was able to find a pen and an old envelope in the glove box. I scratched the address "1401 Sam Austin Drive" on the envelope and scribbled down the time as well.

This neighborhood was crammed with big old houses but they were all in various stages of disrepair. I had not planned on a long stakeout but here I was, and I really didn't want to leave until after Travis did. Specifically though I wanted to see if anyone else I might recognize arrived or left the house while Travis was in it. Things didn't work out as well as I had hoped though. I mean it was Sunday afternoon. Perhaps Travis was in that big old house just watching football with a co-worker. It could be completely innocent. In addition, the clouds were clearing and children were starting to pop out of the houses and soon the hood was alive with curious young people. Not a very good way to stay stealth. Besides, I still needed some groceries. After about an hour I abandoned my quarry and headed to the store.

CHAPTER-12.

I had a bit of a dilemma. It was Sunday afternoon. We had a date with Mandy to go over more of the players luds on Monday night. I really didn't have many other clues to go over at the time, and I really did not wish to get back in touch with Billy Joe and lie about my progress, or lack there of, on the case I was supposed to be working for him. I also did not wish to see Betz and hear her bitch about being cooped up or lament about her friend Anne D'Lorna. I guess I could have just taken the rest of the day off but I was quite restless. The only new clue I had at the time was the house on Sam Austin Drive that I had seen Solter go into. It should not be too hard to track down some information on that piece of property. Even though it was a Sunday the internet works 24/365.

It took a little cyber-surfing before I found the Tarrant County, Texas web site that listed the registered property owners. Once on the site I found that 1401 Sam Austin Drive was owned by one Jeff Watley. By going over my notes I reminded myself that Watley was the real estate agent that Billy Joe had called that fateful day and he was a bit crooked with a record which had him never found guilty but often suspected. O.K. that was interesting. I had witnessed one of the players walking into the house owned by another of the players. These two were now connected. Perhaps their connection ran through Billy Joe, perhaps it did not, but it was starting to look like they were all in on it together. I dug a little deeper into my notes and found that Watley owned a house in Irving and he and his family lived there. According to my internet searches Watley did not own any other property in either Dallas or Tarrant counties. The question going through my mind was "Why would Watley need such a nice big house in that neighborhood?" I mean if he had a girlfriend he was putting up he would need an apartment or much smaller house.

I continued my search and eventually wound up on the website that had the home owner's insurance held by the owner of 1401 Sam Austin. Nothing special there, it was pretty standard stuff for home owners insurance. One more search though hit pay dirt. Home owners insurance would cover re-building the house if there were a fire or something, but it would not cover the contents of the house. When I searched for the policy on the contents at 1401 Sam Austin I found a huge policy but it was not paid by Watley, it was paid by Travis Solter. That meant that Travis was renting the property from Jeff.

I still didn't fully understand what "options" meant in real estate terms but if I had it correct in my mind, Travis was renting a house from Jeff but Billy Joe could decide whether the house got torn down so a mini-mart or parking lot could be built once the new stadium was constructed. I still didn't know exactly who would get the money if the property were sold as stadium fodder but I knew it was not Travis Solter. Still this tied the three bad boys together in some sort of business venture.

Again I reminded myself that all of this could be totally innocent and just a big coincidence, but, in my line of business, we really do not put much faith in coincidences. I needed a good look inside that house to see what they were actually using it for. By now it was 3:30 in the afternoon. I mixed myself a big glass of rum and diet Coke and turned on the Cowboys game. I ordered myself to have just the single drink with rum in it because tonight I did definitely not want to be impaired.

By 10:30 Sunday night I was dressed in black. Black running shoes, black socks, black jeans, a black stretch long-sleeved turtleneck, I even had a black watchman's cap to cover my hair but I had not put that on yet. I had a small black revolver in a shoulder harness that would require me exposing my left breast if I drew it from under my shirt with my right hand, but if I had to draw it, modesty would be the least of my problems. I guess I could have put on a bra but I didn't have a black one. I stuck the six inch razor sharp switch blade in my front right pocket and said a little prayer that I wouldn't accidentally depress the switch while I was driving. I stuck a small penlight in my left front pocket. I made sure my cell phone was on silent but fully charged. I was not planning on using it to call anybody but it would be a much easier camera to use then my good digital. The picture quality would really suck, but it fit neatly into my right ass pocket. I shoved three twenties in the pocket with the penlight not figuring on needing it but feeling safer for having it with me. I took the key to my Taurus off my key ring, and I was ready.

In my driveway I opened the trunk and put the rest of my key ring there for safe keeping. It was dark outside by now of course. Cool but not cold. Quiet.

Not even much noise from the expressway running by my house with the traffic from the Cowboy game long gone and Monday morning's commute several hours in the future. I had not a single speck of identification with me so my main goal right at the minute was to arrive at the Sam Austin house without getting pulled over, therefore I obeyed all traffic laws like it was my first day with a learner's permit.

I exited Brown Trail and had a little trouble finding my way into the neighborhood. All did not look the same as it had ten hours ago when the sun was lighting my way. Still I knew about where the street was so all I had to do was cruise up and down the streets and look at the street signs.

I parked across the street from the house leaving the Taurus un-locked incase I had to make a quick exit from the neighborhood. I rolled down my window even though it was quite cool outside. I wanted to give my eyes plenty of time to adjust to the light level in the area before I got to work, so I sat there and looked and listened for about ten minutes. It was a two story house. There were lights burning on the first floor but none on the second. I could occasionally see blurry movement in the house which indicated that some sort of shades or blinds were drawn. I hoped they would leave me enough room to peek through. I could hear faint music but it appeared to be coming from my side of the street rather than from the house I was peering at. My first move had to be quick. My dome light would blink on when I opened the door and it would stay on until I closed the car door. I wanted to get out of the car as quickly as I could so that I could minimize the time the light was on but I did not want to slam the door making noise. I jumped out and closed the door as quickly as I dared. I stood outside the car for a full two minutes but did not notice any extra movement or noise coming from the house.

There was a large picture window and three smaller windows on the first floor facing the street but as I got closer I could see that the drapes fully covered these portals so I would not be able to see in through any of them. I followed the driveway down the right side of the house and found a window that I could peek in to. It had what we now call mini-blinds but the third slat from the bottom was turned backwards leaving the tiniest gap for me to see through. In my business one never knows what one might see when peering through a window so I tried to prepare for what might be disturbing. Sometimes, of course, when one peers through a window slit, one might see a serene setting where two kids are sitting at the table doing their home work while dad sits watching the news and mom finishes up the dishes. Sometimes, of course, one will simply see nothing at all. This was not one of those times.

I knelt on the cold concrete of the driveway so that I could get level with the gap of light coming from the window. When I peered in I saw a long table that had ten chairs surrounding it. Nine of these chairs were occupied. Each filled with a woman sitting at the table all working together on some project. Several clues told me they were packaging either cocaine or heroine. The first clue was that there were several large trays filled with some white powder. The second clue was that the women were placing measured spoons full of the powder into tiny plastic baggies. A third clue was that the women were all naked except for a shower cap covering their hair. A final fourth clue made itself clear when I noticed the two fully dressed well armed men guarding the women. They did not seem to be concerned with security, rather they appeared to be encouraging the women to work diligently. One thing though really disturbed me, and that was that the women were all beauties. I mean one rarely qualifies for drug work based on physical appearance.

It was a fascinating scene but I could not kneel here all night watching. Every single second I stayed was one more chance that I might get caught. Slowly I stood up. I continued down the driveway toward the back of the house praying that I did not bump into a pit bull or two. I found a second window I could peer through but that view just showed me an empty kitchen. There was a porch along the back of the house which had a small roof. If I could get to that roof I might be able to see into the rooms along the back of the second story. There was a tree growing right where I needed it so I put my athletic abilities to the test and quickly climbed the tree to the roof. The blinds on this second floor were not so cleverly closed and allowed me to see pretty much into the rooms. I was able to see two bed rooms and one bath room. The bath room was quite unremarkable. The window itself into the bath room was tiny and I am quite sure I could not have fit through it.

The bedrooms would have pleased the Marquis De'Sade. Each room held three sets of bunk beds. They were plain metal bunk beds with simple mattresses on each. There were no sheets, no pillows, just six bare mattresses. There were clearly visible manacles at the head and foot of each bed. They could sleep a dozen women in these two rooms. One further thing I noticed was that heavy chicken wire had been nailed over the windows from the outside of the house. Clearly no one would be able to easily sneak out one of the windows.

None of the beds were presently occupied so there was nothing further for me to learn. Quietly I climbed back down the tree and as I dropped to the ground I found myself just five or six feet away from one of the male guards who happened to be standing on the back porch smoking a cigarette. Apparently I surprised him more than he surprised me. By the time he moved I was half way down the driveway running for my life. He shouted something I didn't listen to, and I heard the crack of gun fire. I did not feel any pain or hear the buzz of a close miss, so I kept running for my car. I yanked the key out of my pocket three steps from my car and jumped in. Just as I fired up the Taurus the second guard burst out of the front door and shouted "stop!" like he actually thought I might stop just because he said so. As I threw the Taurus into gear and hit the gas I heard more gun fire and this time I also heard a couple of loud pings. I turned three random corners wheels squealing before I dared put the head lights on.

As soon as I got to a business district I found an open restaurant and pulled into the well lit parking lot. I oriented the car so that I could see anyone entering the parking lot. I pulled out my cell phone and got Detective Samuels on the line. He told me he would have two unmarked cars in the neighborhood in just a few minutes and I didn't question him about jurisdiction.

I stepped out of the car to inspect the damage. I had gotten really lucky because my trusty steed had two new wounds. One was in the passenger door, and the other was in the rear quarter panel. It had only missed the rear tire by a few inches and I couldn't see how it had missed the gas tank unless my understanding of where the gas tank was located was faulty. I did check but there was no leaking fuel.

I slowly drove home forcing myself to concentrate on my driving rather than what I had seen. Once inside I sat at my desk and furiously wrote notes. I could identify four separate reasons why the women had been working nude. The first, of course, was simply that naked people did not have pockets so the drug packagers would not be as tempted to steal any of the valuable powder. The second was a security measure. I believe they were fairly certain that the women would not run for the door while bare. The third reason was one I had heard at a lecture in a criminology class long ago and that was that when packaging the drugs no matter how careful they were some of the powder would in fact get into the air and that powder that landed on the ladies skin would be absorbed acting as a mild but pleasant depressant which has the effect of calming the workers down and allowing them to concentrate on their work. Additionally they eventually get addicted to the small buzz they get and actually look forward to their next work shift. The forth reason to have the women work naked was the most disturbing of all, at least to me. The guards, as I had said, were well armed. Included in their weapons each held a whip. The women would be encouraged to work hard by lashes to their unprotected backs.

I shuddered as I put my notes away then I took them out again. I had to add one more question to paper. I wrote down "Why were all the women so beautiful?" I had a suspicion, but not an iota of proof, and now that I had bungled the surveillance their guard would be doubled or they would simply close down the operation and move it to another location.

CHAPTER-13.

As dawn broke on Monday morning I pointed the Taurus east on 183 and faced the fiercely brilliant sun until 183 swung south where it merged into route 35E. A few minutes later I was sipping bad coffee in Detective Samuels office. I gave him a full report on the Sam Austin house and what I had seen or thought I had seen. He even sent a forensic technician out to measure the fresh bullet holes in my car. Eric Samuels reported to me that he had the house under watch by two units and they had arrived less than an hour after I had called him the previous night. They had reported nobody going either into or out of the house since their arrival. It was possible, of course, that the suspects had fled the house in that hour between my departure and the stakeout teams arrival. The surveillance teams reported little in the way of movement, but the lights in different rooms had gone on and off. Additionally, a van loaded with a lot of high tech equipment was on it's way to the scene. The equipment included a device that would intercept and record any cell phone activity in the area. They also had a heat seeking camera that would allow them to count the people inside the house without entering the abode. Samuels also told me he had someone working on a warrant for a wire tap if they had a land line, but the judge had not yet signed off on that.

For once crime was actually working in our favor. There had been a rash of home burglaries in the area as of late and it was hoped that the people in the house would think they had just scared off a potential burglar when they were flinging bullets at me. We hoped they would play it off as insignificant and continue business as usual until we were ready to take the house down.

I explained my suspicions to Samuels. It was the beautiful women. If they were simply running a drug house the people packaging the drugs would have been chosen for their ability to work hard. The women I had observed doing the task had all been model gorgeous. I was very sure that they had not been chosen for the task based on their work ethics. The women, all so beautiful, had been assembled for some other purpose, and they were being utilized as drug workers while they were waiting for the event that they were actually gathered for. My fear was that we had stumbled onto a white slavery ring. These women had been gathered together so that they could be sold as sex slaves. Perhaps to an isolated mountain top in Montana, but more likely out of the country. There are many countries on this planet that really do not like the good old U. S. of A. I could just imagine powerful men of those countries enjoying having some of our most beautiful women serving as their sex slaves.

The most difficult and most dangerous part of the deal would be transporting these women from where they had been gathered to the country of their destiny. I had no imagination for how that transportation might work but I was pretty sure the women were working drug duty simply to fill their time and their bosses pockets while they were awaiting their own sale.

We had actually made it quite easy for the slavers. I mean how many pretty young girls arrive every year in New York and Los Angeles just knowing they will make it as an actress or model? How many of these find themselves working as strippers or prostitutes within the year? How many of them then go missing? Of those that are missing, how many are actually reported, let alone found? Of course this was all just supposition on my part. All I had really witnessed was drug packaging. As Samuels said, if you were one of the guards for a drug lord would prefer to guard nude beauties or nude sea donkeys? His argument did not win me over, and I was actually surprised that he gave my speculation much credence.

All of this though, the white slavery theory, even the drug packaging, might have little if anything to do with the two separate cases Samuels and I were working. Samuels assignment was to find the killer of Anne D'Lorna. It was difficult to figure any scenario where she could be tied to a white slavery scheme except that her killers had been very professional and already suspected as being from outside the country. On my part, I was supposed to be finding out why Billy Joe might want to kill his wife Betz. Again it was difficult to figure how either of them could be part of the drug activity or the white slavery ring, but there were actually three things that tied them in. First was the fact that Billy Joe held the options to the property. Second, we had fairly concrete evidence that both Travis Solter and Jeff Watley were tied to the Sam Austin house and I had witnessed Travis entering the edifice. Third, both Travis and Jeff were amongst the four calls Billy Joe had made that fateful day.

Samuels made me a promise that he would let me know when the house would be taken down. I desperately wanted to be in on that bust but I was not a cop so at best I could hope to be an observer. I asked Samuels when it would happen and he assured me that it would go down some time that very afternoon. Finally, as he was sending me on my way, he warned me to stay clear of the area until I was invited in. Shit.

Like a good little twenty-first century citizen I had turned my cell phone off when I had gone into the police station. As I sat in my Taurus getting ready for the trip back to Irving I turned the cell back on and found that I had one missed call and that was from Billy Joe. I decided not to answer him right at the moment and headed home. When I got there I checked my answering machine on my land line and Billy Joe had left a message there as well. His voice sounded calm and sure as it always did, but his words were "Xara, it is important, call me as soon as you can."

I checked the date and time stamp for both my cell and my land line. It was nearly nine A.M. and Billy Joe had tried to contact me right at eight. The cell call had come first but when I had not answered that he had almost immediately tried my home number and left the message. That was an hour ago. I really did not want to talk to him but there was just a slim chance that he still thought I was working for him so I had to respond. I followed his example and called his cell first. He, following my example, did not answer. Next I dialed the phone in his office. Surprisingly his answering machine told me he would be out of town on business for the next several days and invited me to leave a message. I did leave a message but only told him I was responding to his calls.

It would be, I was sure, several hours before Samuels called me in regards to the take down of the drug house. If I could guess the cops would want the bust to go down during day-light hours, but they would get everything ready and then wait until almost the last minute before executing the plan. It would get dark at around 6:45 P.M., so I figured they would get things started around six. That was nine hours away. I knew I would not sleep well, but I made myself go to bed to try to get some rest.

I snuggled in next to Laura who was still asleep. She had not worked Sunday night and she was off for tonight as well, so she had no reason to be awake at this point in time. I set the alarm for 3:00 P.M. not expecting to need it but just being safe. Within minutes I was sound asleep.

I was aroused at noon by some noise in the kitchen. I tossed my robe on and hit the potty. When I reached the kitchen I saw my precious little Laura being all domestic preparing three Cornish hens that she would put in the oven a while later. She reminded me that we had a dinner date with Mandy, and I have to admit I had completely forgotten about that arrangement. I drank a big cup of coffee while I watched my cutie do her Julia Childs impersonation. I explained to Laura that I would be out most of the afternoon but also promised to do my best to get back home by about seven.

I knew I could not just sit there all afternoon so I dressed in my usual work clothes, Jeans and a pull over, and kissed Laura on the cheek, and headed to my trusty Taurus.

I wanted to be close to the action when it happened, but Samuels had made me promise to stay out of the area until he called me. Therefore, I figured I would go to the rental where I had Betz stashed. It was only about four miles from the rental to the Sam Austin house. As I drove south on 360 I had to will my car to not get off at Brown Trail but to go instead down the road a bit to where the rental was.

I found the rental completely empty so I crossed the lawn and knocked on Dutch and AJ's door. Dutch welcomed me in and filled me in on everyone else's whereabouts. AJ wanted to get some Easter decorations for their house so she and Betz along with the two guards Tiger and Zebra were headed to the new Ikea store. It would be a long and expensive afternoon. It was though just about perfect for my purposes. Arlington, and the action I was expecting that day was straight west of Dallas, and the Ikea store was in a northeast suburb. Betz would be well guarded and quite far from the action. Dutch handed me a can of diet Coke and escorted me into his crowded office. We sat there and chatted for a couple of hours while he worked at his computer console on some project that I couldn't figure out and was excessively uninterested in. Stashed on a small shelf almost completely buried from view, and turned down in volume so that one could just barely hear it was a 13 inch TV showing a blurry screen full of big men pushing a football up and down a field. It was a Monday in January, and the playoffs had started. I knew no games were scheduled for Mondays so I asked Dutch about it and he explained he had Tivo'd the game from the day before. I hated to tell him how I already knew it would end.

I knew I could trust Dutch so I talked a good deal to him about the case I was working. It is not like he could really help or anything but I find that by talking out loud about something often helps me figure out what is going on. He listened patiently and even asked the proper question here and there, so I knew he was paying attention, but he appeared focused on his computer monitor and I spent most of the time staring at his back.

Three things happened all at once. The first was that on the television the Cowboys had just punted and were down two touch-downs with the two minute warning of the first half. The second was that I happened to look at my watch and it was 4:00 straight up. The third was that my cell phone jumped to life with a shrill beep.

I opened the flip phone and Samuels got right to the point. He told me that Travis Solter had just arrived at the Sam Austin house driving a big truck that he had backed up to the drive way. It looked like they were going to pack up and run, so it was GO time.

I briefly explained to Dutch and was just about to leave when he told me he was coming with me. I tried to argue but Dutch can be pretty persuasive and I really did not have time to debate the matter with him. We both hopped into his jeep and headed to Sam Austin.

Chaos had broken out in the area. Dozens of cop cars jammed the street directly in front of the house and lots of armed men in black uniforms and helmets were swarming in through the front door. There was screaming and the noise of gun fire. The smell of gun powder permeated the air. We both stepped out of Dutch's car. I wanted to get into the action but there was no reason for Dutch to risk his life so I ordered him to stay with his car. I do not remember drawing my weapon but all of a sudden it was in my right hand as I moved towards the house.

Without a uniform it would be very dangerous for me to approach the front of the house because the swat guys would treat anything but their own as enemy, so I looked to the side of the house. The house next door on the west side had a long driveway that stretched all the way to the back yard and there was only a short chain link fence between the driveway and the house with all the action. I started down the driveway to get a look at what was happening out back from the house.

I got to the back of the house and was squatting down looking through the fence at the back door of the house where I saw no action at all when I was surprised from behind when someone tackled me and my gun went flying. Fighting, slapping, swatting, ignoring painful blows, wrestling around I finally got a brief look at my opponent and saw that it was Travis Solter. He was strong and quick but I am one bad assed bitch. Eventually he had me in a bear hug from the back but that left my right arm free to reach into my pocket and yank out my switch blade. I snapped it open and reached between my legs aiming for the Solter family jewels. I must have hit pay dirt because he screamed and let me go and fell to the ground. When I spun around to face him I also fell to the ground and purposefully rolled away from him. I looked down to see him laying still face down on the ground a large pool of blood spreading out from his waist. I looked up and saw the worst nightmare I could have imagined. Billy Joe Jenton was standing there a briefcase in his left hand and his right hand pointing my own gun right at me.

Billy Joe pointed the gun right at me and said "You know what Xara, you are fired."

As his finger depressed the trigger I heard a loud bang. For just a moment a thought flashed in my brain that you were not supposed to hear the bullet when it got you. Billy Joe crumpled to the ground and as his body fell it unblocked the scene from behind him which showed Dutch standing there in a very military like two handed firing position a smoking Smith & Wesson 38 clutched steadily.

"Thanks" was all I could manage when my breath returned.

"I aimed for his right shoulder" Dutch said, "I hope I didn't kill his ass, we will want him alive to testify."

CHAPTER-14.

Dutch stood down and surrendered his weapon to the swat team members that quickly gathered around us. I offered up my bloody knife and it was slipped into a plastic bag. The action was pretty much over. Now the long plodding slow but necessary police work began. As darkness fell the neighborhood was ablaze with red flashing lights. Several ambulances were needed and even a couple of hearses. Billy Joe ended up in one of the ambulances but Travis Solter wasn't so lucky. I had missed his nut sack which was what I was aiming for but I had sliced right through the main artery running down his thigh. He had bled out in just a minute or so. There were two other dead bad guys and one injured bad guy all inside the house itself. Two of the ladies had sustained minor injuries, and one of the swat team had gotten a face full of broken glass when a window was shot out. The most time consuming part of the entire ordeal was finding something for the nine ladies to wear. There wasn't a single garment in the entire house. The ambulance teams had a couple of hospital gowns they could pass out but eventually some cop radioed in an order for a dozen department of justice jump suits.

More official vehicles were arriving. As we started leaving the area forensic police started gathering. It would be a long night for them. A big armored car arrived to transport the huge amount of narcotics the swat team had seized. The neighborhood was crammed with neighbors all wondering what had happened in their quiet little neighborhood right under their noses.

Two different news vans were set up, one at each end of the street guaranteeing that one could not slip away unnoticed. Cameras flashed and reporters yelled questions as the nine beautiful ladies were loaded into a school bus that had somehow been commandeered and driven to the local Arlington PD. Eric Samuels was there but because it was in Tarrant county he wasn't in charge. He was actually running things though. He assigned a cop to me and Dutch for our "protection" but he was really there so that we could not work on a story together. Both Dutch and I would tell the same story because truth was clearly on our side, but Samuels was being ever the professional. With Dutch driving and our escort in the passenger seat I had to fold my large frame into the back of the jeep. Film at eleven.

At the Arlington PD Dutch and I were sent into a large waiting room and most of the people there were related to the case in one way or another. They had put six uniformed cops in the room as well and given us all instructions not to speak to each other until we had been interviewed.

We had only been in the room a few minutes when Samuels called me into the room he had been given to use with the interviews. Besides Solter and Jenton there had been three other men captured at the Sam Austin house. They had been identified and he ran their names by me just to see what I knew about any of them. The injured guy and one of the dead ones had names I had never heard before but the third guy was named Stanley Rand. I wish I had had my notes with me but from memory I was able to tell Samuels that Rand was one of the four names from the list of people Billy Joe had called when this whole mess started and Betz had overheard the death threat. I admitted to Samuels that I had not interviewed him yet and knew precious little about him.

Samuels reminded me to not talk to the other people because he was not even close to through with me, but he sent me back to the bull pen. When I got back there I started thinking about how things had progressed. I had gotten a list of four names from Mandy when the case had started and now three of the four names had all been involved. The fourth name Mandy had given me was that of Aaron Wilson who was the guy who did lawn care for the Jentons and many of their neighbors. I really did not think he was involved. I honestly believe Billy Joe had just called him to schedule yard work but happened to pick that day to call. Anyway, so here I was thinking of the very valuable list of names I had gotten from the luds Mandy had supplied me with and my brain burst out a message to me that poor Laura was at home this very moment cooking Cornish hens for the dinner date I had arranged for Mandy that night at 7:00. I looked at the clock on the wall and it said 7:30. I yanked my cell out of my back pocket and quickly dialed my home number.

Laura was livid. She was not mad at me for being late but she had happened to have the TV on and the news was running the story as one of it's major news events of the day. There had been a piece of film of me and Dutch being escorted to his jeep. So she was real mad that I had not called earlier. When I explained where I was and what I was doing she calmed down a bit. Mandy was already there so Laura put her on the line so that I could apologize to her personally. I told Mandy that her information had been very valuable and, in fact, it was. If I had not had Travis Solter on my watch list I never would have followed him the day he passed me on the highway, and it was then that I had located the Sam Austin house. Mandy was quite impressed with herself but begged me not to tell anyone her name because she would quickly be fired if it were found out she had given me the information to start with. My lover and my friend both promised to have a nice evening without me.

Since we were on the news I figured I better call Betz. I reached her at the rental. She was being guarded at the time by Zebra and the fourth guard who had been added. He went by Rhino and I had not met him as yet. Not surprisingly Ms. AJ was also with them. Betz didn't freak out like I expected. She actually took things pretty well. One thing she did though that I hadn't even considered was that she asked what was being done with her children. She wanted, of course, to drive over to their house immediately and collect the kids. I warned her not to leave the rental and made her promise not to call them either until I called her back. I made enough noise with the cops around me that they finally interrupted Samuels so that I could talk to him. He made a couple of calls and found out the status. They already had a couple of squad cars sitting outside the Jenton home waiting for a warrant to search the place. He arranged for one of the squads to collect the kids and drive them over to their mother at the rental house.

I was interviewed twice in about an hour. Once it was just talking and taking notes with a detective from Tarrant County. The second was with the same detective and an assistant and this one was also videotaped. Dutch also had given his account a couple of times and the clock kept creeping forward. Each time I was led back to the bull pen there were fewer people there. The ladies we had rescued were being interviewed one at a time and when their interviews were done they were taken somewhere else that I didn't know about. Finally Dutch and I and two uniformed cops were all that were left.

Dutch was first to talk to Samuels. He was in there almost an hour. When he came out they had released him to go home so I was saying good bye and thanking him for saving my ass but he wouldn't leave without me reminding me that my car was in his driveway and I would need a ride from the PD to his house.

It was somewhere between Monday night and Tuesday morning when I got my final interview of the evening. Samuels and I sat in the interview room and we both just sat there looking tired for a while. Eventually, with fresh cups of bad coffee, I went through my version of the events. Samuels took almost no notes because he had already heard my story from the other interviewers. My story done, he started filling me in on some of the things that he had learned throughout the night.

Billy Joe and the other injured bad guy were both recovering at the hospital and their injuries were not serious. Both also were singing like birds hoping to get some sort of deal. My supposition was pretty much correct. They had been gathering up good looking but available women and shipping them to the drug dealers in Columbia as pets or sex slaves or what ever they wanted them to be. In exchange they got tons of money. Billy Joe tried to pin the whole thing on

Solter and claimed that it had been he that Billy Joe was talking to when Betz had overheard the death threat, but, of course, he had an explanation for that. According to Billy Joe, he had told Travis that Betz knew about the property in Arlington and Solter wanted her taken out so that she couldn't spoil the deal. Also according to Billy Joe, Travis had wanted to make Betz one of the slaves they were about to ship out so Billy Joe claimed he told Travis he was going to have Betz killed simply to keep him from kidnapping her and selling her in Columbia. Of course, it was quite easy for Billy Joe to suggest these things because Travis Solter could no longer dispute the words and Billy Joe knew that.

From several of the women a pattern of them gathering the women up was figured out. Here is where one more part of the mystery came together. Anne D'Lorna was not quite so innocent as she appeared. Several of the women had been recruited through the charities by D'Lorna. After she had their applications and photos she would turn them over to Billy Joe so that he could identify women who would not be missed if they disappeared. He would then make contact with them and even ended up bedding several of them. They would show up for a date with Billy Joe, get filmed in his bedroom, and a few days later they would be grabbed in their homes in the middle of the night and sent to the Sam Austin home. It was still speculation on our part but Samuels thought the Columbians had probably approached D'Lorna to get her to give up Travis and Billy Joe and cut them out of the deal expecting D'Lorna to recruit the sex slaves for a good deal less money than they were getting.

Samuels though actually was not so sure now that it was even people from out of the country that had murdered D'Lorna. He did not yet have any DNA reports tying anyone to the crimes there, but there were definitely three bad guys tied together at the Sam Austin house and the evidence suggested that three men had caused the D'Lorna carnage. Then Samuels reached into a box and removed an item to show to me. Inside a clear plastic box was the missing liter stein from the set I had seen on Anne's buffet. He told me it had been recovered at the Sam Austin drug house and definitely tied the two crimes together. He told me he did not yet know what clues the beer mug would produce but sincerely thanked me for pointing it out because it was the type of thing that may have been completely overlooked when going over the evidence at the drug house unless anyone knew to look for it.

Dutch, as he had promised, was sitting in the bull pen waiting for me. I was dead tired but he was juiced on adrenalin. He drove me to his house next door to the rental. We checked in with the guards just to make sure all was well. They did not wake Betz or the kids but assured me they were well protected and sound asleep. Dutch invited me in but I begged off and gave him a big hug. It is nice to have a hero around once in a while.

I mounted the Taurus and headed back to Irving checking the dashboard clock which promised me it would be five in the morning before I got home. As I drove I started thinking about my accomplishments now that the case was solved. The actual charge I had when I accepted the job just a week ago was to keep Betz alive until she could divorce Billy Joe or be permanently safe from him. Well she was alive and uninjured as were her children. Billy Joe would be in prison for a long time and the first thing he would learn there is that a divorce to an inmate runs through the court system quickly and smoothly. Secondly, I had accidentally exposed not only a white slavery ring operating right here in Texas but shut down a major drug supplier in the bargain. There were nine beautiful young ladies who had been kidnapped and abused and used as drug workers but I had been instrumental in their rescue and it was mostly due to me that they would be able to put the ugly past behind them and continue on with their lives. One other thought occurred to me. In the contract Betz had gladly signed I would get eight percent of whatever she got from Billy Joe in the next year. I really had no idea at this time what Billy Joe was worth other than it was real big by my standards. Betz would get most of it and I would get a nice slice of that pie. All that I weighed against a couple of days work and two bullet holes in my trusted Taurus. These were the thoughts that were in my mind as I pulled up and parked in front of my home.

The sun would be coming up any time now. I thought this chapter of my life was about over. There was one more little twist awaiting me inside the house which was dark and quiet. It was, after all, the middle of the night. Quietly I snuck into my office and then up the stairs and into my bed room. It was my house. It was my bed room. It was my bed. There were two women in my bed and I wasn't one of them. Laura woke up just enough to tell me not to freak out but that we would talk in the morning. Mandy woke up just long enough to tell me she was happy I hadn't gotten killed in the shoot out.

I rested until dawn in the guest bed room, but I didn't sleep a wink.